12 Days of Mandy Reno

RenoVations Inc. * 2

REGINA RUDD MERRICK

Chapter 1

December 5

The festive mug crashing to the vintage black-and-white tiled floor of the Clementville Café was the last straw. And it wasn't just a mug. It was a mug filled with hot chocolate. Peppermint hot chocolate.

As if plain hot chocolate wasn't sticky enough.

Mandy Reno was done.

Aunt Roxy, owner of the café, and her daughter Darcy rushed from the kitchen at the sound. "Are you okay, sweetie?"

Mandy looked up at her from her position on the floor, cleaning up the mess. "Something tells me it's just not my day."

The sympathy on Roxy Reno's face was almost enough to let those tears fall, but Mandy could be an adult about this.

Lawyers don't cry. Do they?

The strap of authentic sleigh bells pealed out their welcome before she could elaborate. She'd stayed late the night before to help Roxy and Darcy deck the café last night, and she'd been all about anything Christmas. The bells made her laugh. The poinsettias and twinkle lights did something to the region of her heart that only happened at Christmas.

Today?

Today the happy sound irritated her.

"Hey, Mandy."

Her cousin Lisa Reno and her fiancé Nick Woodward approached the counter.

"Everything okay back there?" Lisa chuckled, then stopped as soon as she saw the dark look on Mandy's face. "I guess not?"

Mandy finished mopping up the sticky residue that she would be avoiding all night if she didn't get it up now. Things were picking up with the early supper crowd. Spray cleaner would have to do.

"Hey, guys." Putting the cleaning products under the counter and changing into a clean apron, she put on the best smile she could, glad there were no mirrors to see her face, and glad she didn't have to put on a front for family. Mandy did not have a "poker face."

She looped the long apron strings around her and tied them in front. "Table or booth?"

Nick looked around the dining room and then at Lisa, who nodded. "How about the counter?"

Mandy gestured to the counter in front of her, pulling out paper place mats and cutlery wrapped in napkins. She knew why they were sitting at the counter. Lisa was going to get the scoop out of her, whether Mandy wanted to talk about it or not.

Lisa climbed on the stool, smiling—she was always smiling these days, seemed like—and winked at Mandy. "Sounds good. Christmas is coming, and we need to compare notes for the big Reno celebration at Grandma and Grandpa's. I'm determined to finish shopping this week."

"Like that's going to happen." Nick squeezed his arm around Lisa's shoulders, causing her to laugh.

There it was. In the pit of Mandy's stomach. The empty feeling that had plagued her all day. She turned away to fill water glasses, and under her breath said, "What's even the point?"

"Did you say something?"

Mandy closed her eyes. *Did I say that out loud?*

She turned, heaving a sigh. "It's nothing."

"When are Uncle Ed and Aunt Christine getting home?"

Mandy set the glasses of ice water in front of them and threw up her hands. "Isn't that the question of the day?"

Lisa's brows dipped, confusion written all over her face. "What do you mean?"

"The devastating mudslide in Brazil was in the same area as the hospital they are helping to build and get organized." Mandy's lips settled in a thin line. "The airport's up and running, but Mom and Dad feel like they need to stay there and help."

"Wow." Lisa's eyes rounded. "We were all relieved when we knew they were okay, but I hadn't thought of that. I guess it's pretty clueless of me to think they could just fly home in the aftermath of that disaster."

Mandy waved off her sympathy. "I know, and I understand why they're staying. Really. If I were in their shoes, I'd do the same thing. They're staying for people who lost everything, and I have so much that I didn't even think about." She tried to put on a happy face. "So, Christmas may look a little different this year without Mom to work her Christmas magic."

She turned to check the door when she heard the bells ring once again, seeing who was entering the restaurant.

"Earth to Mandy."

When Lisa's voice filtered through her thoughts, she felt the involuntary smile on her face. "Hmm?"

Lisa chuckled, bringing Mandy back from wondering why in the world Clay Lacey had not been snatched up.

Somebody was missing out on a great guy.

DIRECTING traffic for the fender-bender at the far end of Crittenden County that included a school bus and an extra-wide soybean head attached to a combine harvester was just one more thing to add to Sheriff Clay Lacey's day. Escorting the funeral procession of a long-time resident took up another chunk of time, and supervising the road crew putting up the Christmas lights around the courthouse, yet another.

It was Friday, and Clay was tired.

When he drove through Clementville on his way home from the bus incident, the Clementville Café beckoned.

Pulling up to the brightly lit café, his heart lifted a little. The bell jingled as he opened the door. Looked like since yesterday someone had replaced the regular bell with a sleigh bell strap, giving the sound a definite Christmas vibe. Between that, the staff wearing Santa hats, and the twinkling lights strung on everything, the place defined Christmas cheer.

Garland and greenery lined the windowsills, and there was a huge poinsettia next to the cash register. He lifted a hand to greet Roxy, behind the counter, and Lisa Reno and Nick Woodward, who'd turned at the sound of the bells.

"Hi, Clay. You by yourself tonight?" He looked down, surprised to see Mandy Reno standing before him, picking up a bundle of silverware and waiting for his answer.

"Just me. How are you, Mandy?" Usually, Mandy was a

take-no-prisoners kind of waitress. She was quick, intuitive, and always ready to make suggestions. Tonight, she didn't quite seem herself, Santa hat notwithstanding.

"I'm good. Roxy was nice enough to give me a shift so Darcy could drive into town." She smiled briefly and seated him at a small table, handing him a menu. "Tonight's special is the fish fry, and we have chocolate fudge pie and ice cream in desserts, along with our usual apple and cherry pies."

Something was off.

Clay had known her all her life, and a subdued Mandy was not what he expected this close to Christmas. He narrowed his eyes and looked at her until she raised her eyes to his. "Everything okay?"

Mandy met his eyes briefly, her color rising. "Sure." She took a deep breath and looked away for a split second. "Mom and Dad won't be able to get home for Christmas."

Was that a gleam of tears in the eyes of the girl he'd come to think of as a "warrior princess"?

"I'm sorry to hear that." What could he do? He'd never felt quite as helpless in the face of female tears.

She sniffed and shook her head, giving him what he thought was her brave face. "I'll be fine. I just talked to Mom before I came in to work, so it's still fresh." She shrugged, quietly chuckling. Clay knew she was trying to tamp down emotions. "I'm too old to worry about Christmas. As long as the littles have a good time, I'll live."

"The 'littles'?"

She grinned. "That's what I call my nieces and nephews, collectively. There are four of them, you know, and one on the way. Sometimes it's easier to lump them in one category."

They laughed together.

"Your family's been prolific, that's for sure." Clay smiled, noticing the way her dark hair swept back from her face. Until recently, he hadn't thought of her as a young woman. Five years his junior, she was always Lisa's cousin, or Cassie and Rob's little sister. A kid.

"Yeah, well, I love them to death, but I'm certainly in no hurry to add to the mix."

"You've got plenty of time." He looked down at the menu, not seeing it. For some reason, he felt uncomfortable with the turn in the conversation.

"Not to hear my sister talk. By the time she was my age, she had one child and one on the way." She put a hand on her hip. "Now let me ask you, is twenty-four considered an old maid these days?"

His heart jolted a little. She was twenty-four? That's like— like a grownup.

He looked up at her. Where did little Mandy go? And who was this beautiful young woman before him?

"I would say definitely not."

"Thank you, kind sir." She curtsied and smiled down at him, making his whole week. "Now, what can I get you to drink?"

Something cold, for sure.

MANDY WAS PREOCCUPIED when she came back to the counter to pour Clay's tall glass of sweet tea.

She glanced across the dining room to the table for one. She'd always found the sheriff handsome, and he didn't look all that old. What was he? Twenty-eight? Twenty-nine?

Not exactly ready for Social Security.

His blond hair had just enough curl to be interesting, although he kept it so short, she could hardly tell there was any. The five o'clock shadow wasn't bad, either. The fact that he was Lisa's ex didn't play into how she thought of Clay. Honestly, she loved Lisa's fiancé, Nick, but before he came on the scene she couldn't understand why Lisa didn't fall for Clay. The poor guy pursued her long enough. Didn't that give him "dibs"? And did he still carry a torch for Lisa?

Not my problem.

The overflowing sweet tea running down her hand got her attention, and she shook her head, irritated. What was wrong with her? She emptied the glass and rinsed her hands, then fixed another one so it wouldn't be sticky. That gave her enough time to tamp down the blush she was sure had flamed onto her cheeks.

Mandy walked to his table, setting his glass of iced tea in front of him. "Here you go."

"Thanks." He smiled gently.

"You're welcome. Have you decided what you want?"

"I'll go with the flow and order the fried fish dinner." He gave her the menu and shook his head. "I don't know why I look at the menu. I should have it memorized by now."

"One of these days Roxy and Darcy are going to throw you a curve ball."

"Anything they cook is going to be good, so bring it on." He laughed.

Her heart felt a little lighter. She was still aggravated at her parents and the world in general, but talking to Clay was fun. When she worked as a waitress in the summer, the café had usually been busy when he came in, but tonight, for a Friday night, it was slow.

Her mind was divided between why she'd never really given him the time of day, except in passing, and his order.

Stop it, Mandy. He probably still thinks of me as a kid. Most people around here do. Get it in gear, girl.

"Do you want the works? Beans, slaw, hushpuppies?"

"You bet. It's been a long day."

"Tell me about it."

Clay looked up at her, his face deadpan. "I would, but then I'd have to shoot you. Ongoing investigations, and all." He lifted one eyebrow.

"Very funny." She found herself smiling back at him, feeling the heat rise again. She needed to get away before she did something stupid like spilling his drink on his lap.

Great, Mandy. Put that out into the universe.

"I'll get your order in, then get you some more tea."

"Perfect. I was thirstier than I thought."

Mandy turned to add Clay's ticket to the order wheel, then grabbed his glass and filled it, adding a little ice to the freshly brewed iced tea.

"Thanks." When she handed him the glass, glad to have it out of her jurisdiction, he took another sip and looked her in the eye. "I'm sorry you got bad news."

She shouldn't talk about family matters, but she needed to vent. Lisa was too involved with her engagement to be much help, and her best friend Caryn was so enthralled with her new boyfriend Ben that she was only seeing rainbows and unicorns.

Love. What was that all about, anyway? But here was Clay. She'd known him, literally, all her life. Solid, dependable, seeming to have all the time in the world, Clay. Maybe he would be a good sounding board.

"It's hard to imagine having Christmas without Mom." Even as she said it, she thought she sounded like a cranky teenager, which is probably how Clay looked at her. "Anyway, it'll be fine. I'll be fine." She took a deep breath and raised her eyebrows as if that would lift her sagging spirits as well.

"Ed and Christine are in South America, aren't they? Didn't they have some kind of natural disaster close to them?"

Mandy nodded. "Mudslide. Mom sent pictures. It was

horrible. Mom said so many lost their homes in the mudslide that they opened up the new hospital early, as a shelter, housing the homeless as well as the sick and injured."

He shook his head in sympathy. "That's rough."

"They could come home, but they're needed there." She felt her resolve crumbling and pulled herself up.

Oh no you don't. Don't you dare cry.

"And they're probably just as upset as you are." Clay scrunched his nose.

Why was he being so sensible? Didn't he know that she wanted sympathy, not sensibility?

"I suppose." Grudgingly. "Mom sounded kind of sad, but she was hiding it well. It just won't be the same. I mean, this could be my last Christmas living at home, and now I'm not even doing Christmas." She held her hands in front of her. "Who knows where I'll be this time next year?"

"Where are you staying?"

"At my grandparents' house. My parents left a few weeks before I went back to school, so when I came home on weekends, it was easier to stay at my grandparents' house than rattle around in that big house by myself. I never thought about being afraid in my own house until I stayed down that lonely lane for a few nights by myself. At first, it was an adventure, and then, when we had a thunderstorm that knocked out the power, not so much."

She twisted her lips. "On top of that, it hasn't felt right not helping Mom drag out all the decorations. I may complain every year, but it's always been like clockwork. We have Thanksgiving, then the next day take advantage of the Black Friday sales. After we come home and take a nap, we spend the next day and a half switching the décor in every nook and cranny from pumpkins to candy canes." She shrugged. "Not this year. Christmas is pretty much ruined."

Clay tilted his head. "You can't ruin Christmas, can you?"

She looked at him. "I know Christmas will come and go whether I'm ready for it or not. It's just going to take some getting used to."

Buck up, girl.

"I understand." He paused. "Your family is so big, and mine is so small. Most of the time I cover for my deputies so they can be with their families on Christmas."

"That's so sad." Her jaw sagged in surprise that she said it out loud, but her heart hurt for him. She knew he only had his mom and his grandparents, but she'd never really thought about it. Here she was, complaining because Mom wasn't there to make Christmas special for *her* when he didn't have much to look forward to in any given year. "I'm sorry. I didn't mean ..."

He shrugged his shoulders and propped his elbows on the table, speaking quietly. "It's no big deal. It's just the way things are. We spend Christmas Eve together, then it's pretty much over for us." He looked into her eyes. "But you? You deserve to have a special Christmas."

She paused for a moment, caught in his gaze, feeling a little out of sorts. Was she really that petty? "No, I really don't. I know I'm being a baby about it."

She and Clay both heard the sleigh bells ring and glanced toward the door. Clay gave a nod and wave, and a smile crossed Mandy's face when she saw her other boss, Darcy, rush in with a quick, "I'm back!"

"Better get busy. Thanks for listening, Clay. I'll check on your order."

"Any time, Mandy. I'm in no hurry."

Chapter 2

Clay pondered Mandy's problem while he anticipated his fish dinner. Without fail, the filets would be fried perfectly, flaking just the way good catfish should. Somewhere, some fancy restaurant was missing out not having Roxy and Darcy cook for them.

But then there was Mandy. He glanced up, watching her flit from table to table with her tea pitcher and coffee pot. What would it be like to have a family so close, so devoted to one another, that when even one member was out of pocket, it made a world of difference?

He had the spark of an idea, but he wasn't sure how to go about it. He didn't want to barge in where he wasn't welcome.

Mandy's situation was none of his business. Besides, she would probably think it was strange if he expressed interest in her. Was it strange? Five years wasn't as much of an age gap as it used to be.

He wasn't sure where this was coming from, but one thing he did know—he needed to take it slow.

To his knowledge, Mandy wasn't one to have a boyfriend

hanging around all the time, but then he hadn't been around her since he dated her cousin, Lisa. He looked at his phone, noting the date. Two and a half weeks to Christmas. Twenty days.

That gave him about a week to put together Operation Mandy's Epic Christmas.

MANDY RUBBED her elbow where she whacked it against the counter, stopping at her cousin's knowing grin.

"Slow down, we're in no rush." Lisa laughed. "Don't tell me you got a bit of the Reno klutz gene, too?"

"What?"

"Nothing." Lisa raised her brows.

Wait a minute. Was she blushing? Her face had to be glowing, it was so warm. She couldn't help herself. She glanced toward the table where Clay was sitting, hoping he hadn't seen her awkward moves.

Stop it, Mandy Lou.

She flashed her eyes at her cousin, trying to send her a message telepathically. She was trying to tamp down her freckle-faced blush. "Don't you think it's a little warm in here? The ovens heat the place up better than the heating system."

Apparently, telepathy did not run in the Reno family as much as awkwardness.

Lisa did not get the silent message and arched a brow. "Feels fine to me, but we just came in from the cold." She tilted her head a little, narrowing her eyes. "Seemed pretty cozy with Clay over there."

"Stop it. Clay was just being nice to me." Mandy handed them their menus and glanced over at the gentleman in question, smiling when he glanced over at her. Now she was self-conscious. Time to change the subject. Quickly.

Nick nodded. "He's a nice guy."

"I agree." Mandy stuck her tongue out at Lisa, then chuckled. Her load was lighter, for sure.

"Better watch it, your face'll freeze like that!" Lisa shook her head. "I'm sorry about your mom and dad. That's tough. What did Grandma have to say about them not getting home in time for Christmas?"

"Oh, you know Grandma. She always looks on the bright side. Said we'd make it fine, that she was glad to have some help dragging out the Christmas decorations this year."

Lisa chuckled. "I'm sure Grandpa is happier about that than Grandma."

"Right?" Mandy sent her cousin a genuine smile—her first of the day—and then it drooped. "I was looking forward to having them home, and who knows? This may be my last Christmas to live at home."

"Are you done with your semester?" Nick drained his glass and held it out for more, Mandy filling it before he could say a word.

"I've got two papers due at the end of the week, then I should get my grades next week." She felt a little shiver. "Prepping for the bar exam will be next."

Lisa shook her head. "You'll be fine."

"I'm not big on surprises. Shouldn't you be able to plan for almost any eventuality?"

"Sorry, Mandy. And welcome to the real world." Lisa elbowed her fiance and chuckled. "I certainly didn't plan for *this* one to come back into my life, and look at us now."

"Being a grown-up stinks sometimes." Mandy twisted her lips, embarrassed. "Grandma called me on it, though."

Lisa grinned. "What did she say?"

"You know Grandma. She called me Amanda Lou and gave me her sermon in a sentence."

The two young ladies each straightened their spine, quoting their grandmother verbatim. "We don't know what the future holds, but we know Who holds the future."

Mandy shrugged. "It's right up there with 'pretty is, as pretty does.' I guess that means it'll be up to Grandma and me to make Christmas for the rest of the bunch. We'll be a little smaller group this year anyway since Uncle Tom, Aunt Ginger, and their crew aren't coming down until New Year's."

"Let me know how I can help." Lisa glanced over at Nick. "Aunt Christine has always been the Christmas elf in the family."

He laughed. "Oh?"

Mandy nodded. "Really. You've heard the phrase, 'Christmas threw up in here'?"

Nick laughed, and Lisa snorted a little.

"Oh, yeah. Mom can make an over-the-top Christmas out of paper plates and dollar store garland and have it look like something out of *Southern Living*."

Lisa bounced on her stool. "She's right. One year, she created a 'Candyland' that started at the end of the sidewalk and reached into every room in the house." She leaned into her fiancé and grabbed his arm. "She even found candy-striped bathroom tissue. TMI?"

"And don't forget the year of the snowmen." Mandy's heart was feeling lighter already. "She had dozens of them. And to top it all off, she had us out there spreading biodegradable fake snow on the grass right before the family arrived. It was seventy-five degrees with a chance of thunderstorms that year, and we had to wait until the last minute to put it out, in case it rained." She grimaced a little. "Remember the bigger-than-life-sized snowman that greeted everyone at the door?"

Lisa's guffaw came out unexpectedly, and she clapped her hand over her mouth as she looked around at all eyes on her and Nick shaking his head in mirth. "Sorry. I'll try to keep it down. That snowman was just creepy. I haven't felt the same about snowmen, since—and don't get me started on Frosty."

Mandy nodded, matter-of-factly. "You know where I stand on the Frosty issue. Same."

Nick looked from one female Reno to the other. "Frosty?"

The girls exchanged glances and nodded in tandem.

Lisa began. "Have you ever wondered about the trauma those kids were subjected to when a snowman—*a snowman*—came to life?"

"And," Mandy continued, "how selfish little what's-her-name—"

"It was Karen." Lisa turned to Nick. "You can't say we don't know our holiday cartoon characters."

"Noted." Nick shook his head and smiled into his tea glass.

Mandy nodded. "Oh yes. Anyway, how selfish was it for her to expect Frosty to take her into a greenhouse? I always thought it made no sense whatsoever. Hello? Melting?" She snorted. "On top of that, what was she thinking following a snowman that far from home, anyway?"

Nick frowned, scratching his head. "Never really considered evaluating 'Frosty, the Snowman' from a realistic perspective."

"Well, now you have." Lisa leaned on the table toward him. "We take these things very seriously in the Reno family."

"A familial group of critical-thinkers ... Sounds like I'm getting into the right family." Nick chuckled.

"You have no idea. Wait until you hear our analysis of *Gilligan's Island*." Mandy looked up as the sleigh bells chimed once again. "I'll be back in a minute to refill your drinks."

"Thanks, Mandy."

She left Nick and Lisa perusing the menu and waffled over whether to seat the next customers or heed the ding that meant "order up!" It was probably Clay's order since he was having the special tonight. Her decision was made when Darcy came in and greeted the newcomer.

Chapter 3

Clay observed as Mandy talked to Lisa and Nick. She seemed to be feeling better if her laughter was any indication. He knew Mandy and her cousin were close.

He scrolled through his phone, deleting junk emails containing sales for items he'd never buy because he didn't have anyone to shop for outside his small family.

But the idea he'd had earlier was beginning to gel. He closed his email app and opened up his Internet app, punching *"The Twelve Days of Christmas" lyrics* into the search bar to remind himself of the items on the traditional list of gifts.

There was no way he could replicate that. He saw it done on a television sitcom, and it was hilarious but destructive. Who wants six geese a-layin' for Christmas?

Maybe there would be an alternative. He'd have to think about that. He wasn't sure how long he'd been looking at his phone, but suddenly, there was Mandy with a tray laden with all the fixings of a Fried Catfish Dinner.

"Looks like Roxy has outdone herself." Clay rubbed his hands together in anticipation.

"She cooks the best fish in the area, I think." Mandy arranged the dishes in front of him and then stood back, surveying her work. "Can I get you anything else?"

"Maybe dessert later?"

Her eyes crinkled when she smiled, which was an improvement on her expression, earlier, and he was glad. "I'll check on you in a little bit. Tea holding out okay?"

"I'm good. Thanks, Mandy."

"You're welcome, Clay."

She picked up a pitcher of tea and sashayed between the tables, more confident than earlier. Watching her, Clay resolved, then and there, that Mandy would have a Christmas she would never forget.

Instantly, niggling doubts threatened to make him change his mind. Could he pull it off? What would she think when she learned it was him? Was it a bad idea? Would the attention make her uncomfortable? Would she, and the community in general, take it the wrong way? It wasn't like he had any designs on her.

Did he?

Thrusting the negative self-talk away, he decided it was time for him to take a few chances. *You only live once.*

The next customer that came through the door gave him pause. He didn't think he'd ever seen him before. Glancing at Mandy, he saw her pale.

Clay was on high alert.

WHAT WAS THOMAS DOING HERE?

Maybe he hadn't seen her.

Mandy slid behind the counter, where Darcy was filling some glasses.

"Are you okay?" Darcy's brows gathered as she looked at Mandy.

Mandy glanced over at the new customer. "I think so, but could you wait on table seven?"

"Sure thing." Darcy looked over at the table in question, then back at Mandy, a question in her eyes. "Do you know that guy?"

Mandy nodded. "We dated some in college before I went to Lexington. He showed up back in the summer."

"Not someone you want to be with?"

"Not at all." Mandy took a deep breath. "Let's just say he has a wandering eye. But for some reason decided *he* could wander all he wanted but became a jealous lunatic when I talked to another guy or wanted to plan something with my friends." She glanced toward the table he occupied. "He has a mean streak."

Darcy frowned. "That took 'let's just say' to a whole 'nother level."

"I know. Lawyers can be a wordy breed. Even future ones." Mandy sighed. "I thought the last time he came up here, I made it clear it was over."

"I dated a guy like that once." Darcy looked at her closely. "Be careful. It's not a big jump from nuisance to stalking, and from stalking to assault."

Mandy nodded. "I'll try to avoid him if you can wait on that side of the dining room."

Darcy put an arm around her shoulders and squeezed. "Be glad to." She looked toward Clay. "Might not be a bad idea to show him you're friends with law enforcement." With a raised eyebrow, she said, "Looks like Clay could use some more tea."

Feeling her lips twitch suddenly Mandy felt lighter. Thomas might scare her a little, but as long as Clay was here? With Clay here, she could slay dragons.

And if not? She had a feeling he would slay them for her. She couldn't decide if that image calmed her or excited her, or both.

Either way, his tea glass wasn't going to fill itself.

Chapter 4

December 11

Now that her grades had been posted, Mandy began to relax and anticipate Christmas, with or without her parents. She and her grandparents had practiced FaceTiming with her laptop hooked up to the television, and it had been a success. They could repeat it on Christmas when the whole family was there and it would almost—*almost*—be like having her parents in the living room with them.

She still wasn't completely on board with her Christmas changing so much, but Grandma and Grandpa had done their best to keep her busy. They'd decorated the house, and tomorrow she and Grandma were going to make gingerbread cookies. She couldn't wait. Grandma's were the best, bar none, and this would be the first time since she was a little girl that Mandy had been around during the baking process. She was determined to learn Grandma's secret.

After some thought and consultation with her siblings, they came up with a theme for their Christmas celebration this year—An Old-Fashioned Reno Christmas. Mandy brought Mom's old photo albums to Grandma and Grandpa's house, and they'd each picked an era in their family's life to showcase on Christmas Day. Everyone in the family had their assignment, and everyone had promised to keep it as authentic as possible.

So far, Mandy was as busy as she'd ever been this close to Christmas. Between picking up odd shifts at the café and helping Lisa with a couple of decorating jobs, she didn't have much time to sink into despair.

She didn't tell Grandma about Thomas showing up at the café. Eventually, she'd probably have to face him and tell him, once and for all, that he needed to leave her alone. Darcy and Clay had been her protection last night, but they wouldn't always be there.

A horn honked in the driveway, and Mandy looked up. Lisa. Mandy was going with her cousin on a shopping excursion for a decorating job she was working on. Maybe they could run into the craft mega-store in Paducah while they were in town. Grandma's ribbon stash was getting low. That and Mandy was in the market for some old-fashioned large-bulb Christmas tree lights to string around the front door as part of her 1970s-theme assignment. She'd talked Grandpa into dragging out of the barn the tall plastic illuminated candles that she'd heard her dad talk about being on either side of the door when he was a kid. The electrical cord pulled off as soon as they touched it, so Grandpa, being a grandpa, grumbled a bit, and then said he'd rewire them for her.

She wasn't the youngest grandchild for nothing.

Mandy ran to the door and waved, then raced into the kitchen. "Grandma, I'm heading out with Lisa. Need anything while we're in Paducah?" She always asked, because her grandmother tried to avoid the Christmas crowds as much as possible, and the hour-long drive to town made it less enticing the shorter the days became.

"Hold on a minute. I've got a list." Grandma tore the list from the magnetic tablet on the side of the refrigerator. She kept a list going "just in case" someone was passing through a shopping mecca. If not, she could pick up her supplies at the local grocery. Adjusting her glasses to peer at the list, she looked up at her youngest grandchild, brow arched as she looked at her over her glasses. "Looks like we need more marshmallow cream. Seems to me like we've gone through more batches of fudge this year than usual."

"Why, Grandma, I have no idea what you mean." She laughed and blatantly snagged the last piece of delectable chocolate goodness from the container on the counter. "I'll get two or three jars. It's still two weeks until Christmas."

"Good idea. And if you go to the big-box store, pick up one of those five-pound bags of chocolate chips. At two cups of chips per batch of fudge, it goes fast."

Mandy smiled at the loving smirk on Grandma's face. "Will do. If you think of anything else, you can call me or Lisa." She arched an eyebrow. "Or, you could text me."

Grandma waved her off. "It would be quicker for me to call than to keep going back and forth correcting my mistakes while texting. It's not worth it." She gave Mandy a hug and a kiss on the cheek. "You girls have fun and stay out of trouble."

"Trouble? Lisa and me?" She clasped her hand to her chest in mock horror.

Grandma's smirk was one of those mannerisms that Mandy had inherited. "Yes, you two."

"ARE you feeling better about your mom and dad not being here for Christmas?" Lisa spoke above the Christmas carols playing over the radio.

"Not better, but more resigned." Mandy turned toward her cousin. "Grandma and Grandpa have done everything in their power to make sure I have a good Christmas, and I don't want them to think I don't appreciate what they're doing."

"I get it." Lisa nodded, maneuvering holiday traffic as they eased onto the Interstate. "That first Christmas after Mom died, we didn't want to acknowledge it, but somehow, Grandma made it happen anyway."

"I thought about that. Here I am complaining about my little world being inconvenienced when you've lost Aunt Carol." Mandy's eyes misted. "I'm sorry."

"Don't apologize. Life happens. That was a tough Christmas. But last Christmas? That was the one where Dad and Roxy reconnected. Instant family." Lisa grinned. "We still miss Mom, but Roxy knew her so well that it feels like she's still with us, you know?"

Mandy sighed, staring out the windshield at the oncoming headlights. If she scrunched her eyes and looked at them through her lashes, they almost looked like Christmas lights.

"The worst part was that I found out during finals week. I was already stressed to the max." Mandy looked over with a grimace. "Great timing, huh? Fortunately, I had my papers mostly written." She shrugged. "My grades didn't take too much of a hit, but I'm glad the semester is over."

"I'm sure. By the time I got to the end, I was so over it." Lisa laughed as she shook her head. "And I had two years less to worry about compared to you."

"Be glad. Sometimes I think I made a mistake going to law school, but I've done well, so maybe that's my confirmation."

"Sometimes God gives us talent in lots of things, whether or not He wants us to use it for our livelihood."

"I'd like to use the law to help people." Mandy stared straight ahead, focusing on the flurries swirling on the windshield. "Getting into a big law firm with all the dog-eat-dog competition has never been my goal."

"Do you think you'll stay around here?"

Mandy paused, thinking. Would she? "I'm not sure. I mean, I love the old hometown, but there's not a lot to keep me here beyond all of y'all." She sighed. "Sometimes I think everyone expects me, since I'm in law school, to be all big-city, but it's not me."

Lisa nodded. "I loved living in Texas, but I've hardly regretted moving back home. Well, maybe a little bit, but that was before I started dating Nick." She turned and smiled at her cousin, then sobered. "Of course, I came home because Mom was sick, so that was different, and then Dad." Lisa shook herself. "When Dad had his heart attack, I was glad I was here already. But it's all good, now."

"If that were the case, I'd be here in a heartbeat too." Mandy was quiet for a few seconds. "Enough about me. How's the wedding planning going?"

Lisa stretched her arms out on the steering wheel, threw her head back, and groaned. "*Ugh.* There's so much more to it than I thought. I figured if I could plan an entire house from top to bottom a wedding would be no problem, but there are so many little details to think about. Dad and Roxy were smart to go simple."

"I guess you and Nick could too."

"I know. But I don't want to look back and wish we'd done it up big."

"You've got plenty of time."

"That's the problem. When we got engaged, we agreed to a

short engagement, but as everyone started chiming in, it gets pushed further and further away. It's driving us both nuts. We just want to be married."

Mandy laughed. "You could always elope." No way Lisa Reno would buck the system. She knew her cousin all too well.

"Don't think it hasn't been considered." She shook her head as if to clear her mind. "Before weddings can happen, Christmas is going to happen, whether we like it or not."

"Exactly." Mandy took out her list. "I know we're on a work trip, but I may need to make a few stops while we're here."

"Me too. I ordered a few things for the twins that need to be picked up." Lisa kept her eyes on the road but reached down to give Mandy her notebook. "Check the page I have marked. It's a list of the items we need to get for the Adams' project."

Glancing over the bulleted list, she nodded in approval. "This isn't too much. I say we get those things done, then we won't be in a rush for our Christmas shopping."

"You read my mind." Lisa stopped at the first stoplight coming into Eddyville before getting to I-24 and took the opportunity to look across the seat at her cousin. "Mandy? Are you all right?"

When they'd stopped at the stoplight, Mandy had glanced over at the truck in the lane next to them. She thought she'd seen Thomas, but upon closer inspection, it was just a guy with dark hair, and he had a woman in the car with him. "I'm fine." She twisted her lips to one side. She needed to tell Lisa.

"Do you remember Thomas, who came up last summer?"

"I remember. "Lisa cut her eyes to Mandy. "Wasn't he the one you thought you had cut loose?" Lisa frowned. "Is he bothering you again?"

"Maybe."

"No maybe, about it. Either he is or he isn't."

"He was at the café again last night."

"*Again?* You're kidding me. Why didn't you say anything?"

Mandy shrugged her shoulders. "Trying to give him the benefit of the doubt. I mean, he lives in Paducah, so maybe he just likes Roxy's food?"

Lisa laughed out loud. "It's good, but I doubt seriously he drove the sixty miles to Clementville to eat meatloaf."

"I hate thinking I'm so ineffectual that I can't break up with a guy and have it stick." Mandy released a deep sigh. "What kind of lawyer is that?"

"One who is a beautiful young woman with a tender heart." Lisa shook her head. "I'm surprised you haven't had more guys buzzing around you."

"What am I? Scarlett O'Hara, or something?"

"I surely hope not!" Lisa laughed out loud. "You've never considered that you are the pretty one in the family." It was a statement, not a question. "I mean, I had my 'ugly duckling' stage, but you? You never did." She shook her head. "It was a little disgusting. When I was eighteen and you were thirteen, people thought we were the same age."

And now Mandy laughed. "Oh, brother. Definitely time to change the subject." She looked over at her cousin's beautiful auburn hair and smooth skin and knew that while Lisa may have been awkward as a teen, she'd always been gorgeous. To Mandy, anyway.

Lisa chuckled. "Okay, then, what have you been doing for fun?"

Fun? She was in law school. "*This* is fun." Was this part two of the "How's your love life" interrogation? And here she was, trapped with a person who was not only in love but also engaged to be married. Those were the worst.

"You know what I mean." Lisa drove on, setting her cruise control on the four-lane heading toward the Interstate. It was easy to speed there, and it was also easy to get stopped. They'd all had close calls.

"You mean am I dating anybody?" That's it. Get it out there and then nip it in the bud.

"Um-hmm. Anybody special in Lexington?"

"After Thomas, I decided to take a break from dating. Besides, who has time?" She began to relax, looking at either side of the truck at twinkling lights. "Okay, I did go out on a few group dates, but none of them went any further." She shrugged.

Lisa blew out a breath. "Do you ever wonder what it would be like to date the way our parents did? The boy-meets-girl, boy-calls-girl, boy-picks-up-girl, boy-meets-dad, boy-promises-to-get-her-home-early date?"

"That seems like a lot of responsibility for the aforementioned *boy*."

"It does, doesn't it?" She sighed. "But wouldn't it be nice to put it all on them?"

Mandy scoffed. "And a little scary, if you ask me. It just seems like all the guys my age are still kids."

Lisa leaned forward, looking back to check for oncoming traffic, and pulled onto I-24. "I know what you mean. Adolescence lasts longer now, especially if they're still in school. I read somewhere that men's brains don't finish developing until they're twenty-six. And maybe not until they're thirty."

Mandy groaned. "Why am I not surprised? I'd like to be asked out on a real date. You know, like you said earlier, minus the promise to get her home early stuff. I think I can be depended on, at twenty-four, to know when my bedtime is."

Lisa laughed out loud. "I'm sure." She carefully entered the heavier Interstate traffic, sliding into the right lane between an eighteen-wheeler and a large SUV. "We need to find you someone who is at least as mature as you."

"Or maybe more so?"

The girls laughed together, and for some reason a thought flashed through Mandy's mind centered around a certain tall, good-looking, blond sheriff. He was certainly mature enough. Was he *too* mature?

Mandy sat quietly for a few miles, thinking. No, Clay wasn't too mature. Maybe he was just right.

Assuming, of course, that the admiration was on both sides. Who was she kidding? He probably looked at her and thought about twelve-year-old Mandy in pigtails and blue jeans.

Chapter 5

December 14

Twelve days until Christmas, but there were a lot of logistics to pull together between now and then. Clay wasn't sure he could do it. He knew he couldn't on his own.

He walked down the shiny terrazzo floor in the hallway of the 1960s-era courthouse, heading to the County Clerk's office. Most people had plenty to do this close to the holidays, and the halls were empty compared to some days. On court days or election days, activity was high, but on a regular day in mid-December? The custodians were leaning on their mops, and the clerks were waiting for their next customer to take care of business. Renewing license plates, mainly.

"Hi, Clay." Caryn Brown was just the lady he wanted to see.

"Hi, Caryn. How are you?" He gave her the standard greeting, complete with a smile.

On to the business at hand. When your goal is to surprise someone special, who did you call? That someone's best friend. And that happened to be Caryn.

"I'm good. It's slow as molasses around here today."

"I hear you. It's too cold out for anyone to get into any meanness, as well." He laughed.

"I guess that's a good thing." She scrunched her nose.

"I'd say so." He leaned forward and spoke quietly. "Can you come by the office before you leave today? There's something I want to discuss with you."

Her face blanched slightly. "Is everything okay?"

He waved his hands to wipe away her fears. She was dating one of his deputies, his best friend, Ben Lockhart, and he was happy with Ben's choice of female companionship. She was good at her job in the Clerk's office, and he could see her running for the office sometime in the future. "Everything is fine, I just need your advice about something."

Her brows came together in confusion. "My advice?"

He looked down the length of the counter to see if the other ladies were listening to their conversation. If they were, they were doing an excellent job of not looking up, and almost too good a job at not meeting his eyes. Hmmm. Did he see Melinda, in the cubicle next to Caryn, jerk her head around when he looked?

"There's a ... project I'd like your help with if you don't mind. You and Ben both, if possible."

"Okay." She still looked puzzled. "I get off at three, is that okay?"

"Perfect. If I have to go out, I'll leave word with Amy."

She nodded. "I won't forget."

"Thanks, Caryn." He patted the counter, waved at the other ladies, and turned to leave.

THIS WAS the first day that Mandy didn't have something to do. It was easy to relegate disappointment to the back burner when you're waiting tables or hanging wallpaper with Lisa, but the café was closed on Mondays, and Lisa was out Christmas shopping with Nick. With no schoolwork, Mandy was at loose ends. It wasn't like she was lonely ... Or was she?

She and Grandma had finally decorated the house a few days earlier, and everything glistened with Christmas cheer. Maybe not as much as Mom would have done, but Mandy had a feeling that maybe, just maybe, she had inherited the Christmas gene. Fingers crossed, because her sister Cassie did well to get a tree up with her brood.

Grandpa, true to his word, went to the hardware store in Marion and bought a light kit to rewire the vintage outdoor candles.

Now if Mandy just felt a little more Christmas-y. She could finish wrapping gifts, but ...

Mandy grabbed the novel—John Grisham's *Skipping Christmas*—that she'd been reading since classes ended. She could relate to the urge to banish all thoughts of the holiday when things didn't go as planned, but she knew how the book ended, and she needed encouragement. She'd read it at least three times. Today, her plan was to curl up on her end of the sofa and read while Grandpa watched the news. Maybe they could watch a Christmas movie later.

Her phone sounded the ding for a text around 4:30 that afternoon. She picked it up to see who it was.

It was Caryn.

Hey, girl, what's going on?

She didn't see much of Caryn these days, especially since she started dating Ben, but they had grown closer over the summer and fall. Their childhood friendship had blossomed into adult friendship, and it was like they hadn't missed a beat.

Nothing much. Reading, watching TV.

Sounds scintillating.

That's a big word for a text.

Tell me about it. Auto-correct had a field day.

Mandy laughed. Caryn, with her blue eyes, bleached-blonde hair, and black fingernail polish, was as opposite Mandy as could be on the outside, but in the areas that mattered—their faith, the importance of family, and the desire to be there for one another—they were in total agreement.

She looked as she saw the familiar dots indicating Caryn was typing another message.

I have a delivery for you.

Really?

What would she be getting this close to Christmas? Had Mom and Dad sent something? But why would they send it to Caryn?

Yes, and before I get there, I just want to tell you not to ask me any questions. Agreed?

Okay?

Great. I'll be there in 15.

I'll be here. Want to eat supper with us?

Can't. Cooking for Ben. ;)

La-ti-da.

See you, goofball.

Back at ya.

"OKAY, she's in place. Does this covert op have a name?" Caryn pocketed her phone and eyed Clay closely. He had a feeling she wasn't too sure about this whole thing.

"I hadn't thought of one." His brows went down. He should have been prepared for the detail-oriented Caryn to think of every aspect of this as soon as she was informed.

She dismissed it with a wave of her hand. "That's fine. If I come up with one, I'll let you know."

Clay's lips twitched. He should have put her in charge.

"What's going on here? Are you trying to steal my girl, Clay?" Deputy Ben Lockhart stuck his head around the door frame, eyebrows raising when he saw Caryn sitting in the office.

"I might be arresting her, you never know."

"For disturbing the peace?" Ben's eyes twinkled. "She disturbs my peace on a daily basis."

"Oh, you." Caryn didn't embarrass easily, but her face was adorably red at Ben's comment. "We have a mission."

"To ...?"

"To help Clay surprise Mandy."

"Okay, this I gotta hear." Ben made himself comfortable in the second chair across from the sheriff.

Caryn turned back to Clay. "How did you come up with this? And why?"

Clay leaned back in his chair, thinking. Probably scowling. He'd seen his reflection one day when he was pondering something, and he couldn't believe how angry he looked when he furrowed his brow.

He tried raising his eyebrows to lessen the severity of his countenance. How could he explain to this young woman that he was crushing on her best friend? Would she be horrified at the very idea?

And what twenty-nine-year-old man uses the word "crushing"?

"Well?"

He twisted his lips and glanced around. Amy, his receptionist, had left for the day, and the courthouse was practically empty. He looked up, avoiding Ben's tickled expression and having a hard time meeting Caryn's gaze that was focused on him. Too focused. "I want to cheer Mandy up since her parents aren't coming home for Christmas."

"So, let me get this straight," Ben said, clicking his pen as he leaned back and relaxed. "You want to woo Mandy Reno. Robbing the cradle, much?"

"I don't know if 'woo' would be the correct term, here."

"Uh-huh." Caryn looked over at Ben and frowned, shutting him up. "I think Mr. Lockhart here is forgetting that there's almost the same difference in our ages as in yours and Mandy's."

Ben held up his hands in surrender. "Hey, I'm the younger man here. Just sayin'."

She crossed her arms and leaned back in the green vinyl chair across from him. She seemed relaxed. The way a person approaches a wild animal is relaxed, thinking it will help the animal to be less fearful. "Clay Lacey, I've known you since I was a kid."

"Hey, I was a kid too. I'm not that much older than you." *Here it comes. The objection.*

Caryn nodded. "No, you're not, are you? The older we get, the closer in age we are, if that makes any sense. When I was little, you were one of the *older* boys." Then her eyes seemed to look deep into his soul. "You like Mandy. You *do* want to *woo* my best friend."

Why do people with light hair and a light complexion turn red so easily? He could feel the heat rolling off his face, and that was not a feeling he liked.

He studiously avoided Ben, still.

Ben wants to yuk it up. He thinks it's stupid. That I have no chance.

She straightened up in her chair and leaned forward. "Clay, are you in love with my best friend?" Her eyes were round with awe, but she was smiling.

"It's crazy. Forget it. I knew it was a mistake, but I didn't realize how preposterous it sounded until I heard myself say it." He started to stand up before he could spill more personal information. It wasn't worth the ragging he would get. He was embarrassed enough already.

"Sit yourself right down, Sheriff Lacey." She leaned forward as he complied, and shot Ben a look that bade him keep his mouth shut. "Just because it wasn't my idea for you to date Mandy, doesn't mean it's not a good idea. In fact, I don't know why I didn't think about it before." She frowned.

"You think I'm too old for her."

"No, that's not it. It's just that you chased Lisa for years." She paused for emphasis. "And I mean *years.*"

He raked his hand over his face. People were going to think he was insane, or creepy. One or the other. Maybe both. "I know. And I realize now that I was in error the entire time. It just felt like I *should* be in love with Lisa. It was rational. Sensible, even. We fit, I thought." He took a deep breath and forced himself to be calm. "I'm not attracted to Mandy because she reminds me of Lisa if that's what you're getting at."

"No, I hadn't really thought of that." She shook her head.

"Except for that Thomas guy last year—she broke it off with him by the end of the summer—Mandy's not dated much. I've tried to fix her up a few times." She looked at Ben. "She doesn't trust my judgment, for some reason."

Ben coughed. Caryn reached over and took his hand.

"Somebody had to take this one on." She cheesed a smile at Ben, who winked audaciously, and then considered Clay seriously. "But Mandy's different from me. She's serious, she's driven, and she has a plan. I'm not sure that plan includes a small-town sheriff. But I could be wrong."

Who is Thomas?

"If it doesn't go anywhere, that's fine. I just want to do this for her. Whether or not she ever realizes it's me, I'll be watching to see if it makes her happy." He shrugged his shoulders. "That's all." He looked her in the eye, then got up the nerve to look at his friend, relieved to see his attention was all on Caryn. "Will you help me?"

Her slow smile reminded him of the Grinch, for some reason—the *after* Grinch—

after his heart grew three sizes.

"I am so in, you wouldn't believe it."

"Me too." Ben chuckled. "About time you started thinking about yourself."

"Yeah, well." Clay leaned forward, speaking softly. "Can you guys keep the secret?"

"I will do my utmost. Pinkie-swear?" At that, Caryn linked her pinkie to his and picked up the gift bag.

"Ben?"

"I refuse to pinkie-swear, but I give you my word as a gentleman."

"Oh, my." Caryn shook her head in frustration, but her lips were twitching in good humor.

Fluttering her fingers, she picked up the bag and left his office, Ben following close behind.

Clay sat back in his chair, staring into space. Cleared for takeoff. On your mark, get set, go. No turning back. This was really happening.

This will end up succeeding ... or failing spectacularly.

MANDY OPENED the door to a decidedly over-stimulated Caryn. "Hey, come on in."

"I may or may not have speed-ed a little to get here. I couldn't wait to see what's in the bag." Caryn tucked her almost-white curly hair behind her ear.

"Don't you know?" Mandy eyed her suspiciously.

She held her hands up. "I can only say one thing."

"And what's that?"

"It's not me." Caryn gave her a Cheshire cat grin that bade Mandy to not ask any questions because it wouldn't do any good. Caryn had many qualities, and the keeping of secrets was one of them. She was the soul of discretion.

Mandy set the glittering bag on the table about the time her grandmother came through from the kitchen. "What's all this? Early Christmas?"

Mandy looked at Caryn, who couldn't wait to tell what she knew—minus who it was from, of course.

"I think Mandy may have a secret admirer."

"Oh, please." Mandy rolled her eyes in disgust.

"What's in the bag?" Grandma looked as excited as Caryn.

"I was just getting ready to open it." She pulled out the tissue paper and two items, also wrapped carefully in tissue paper. She opened the bulkier object and frowned. "A pear? One lone pear?"

"Open the other one." Caryn began to bounce.

She carefully unfolded the square, flat object. "It's a CD. Who listens to CDs anymore?" She turned it over to see the title and laughed. "The Partridge Family Christmas Album." She looked from Caryn to Grandma, then at Grandpa who had come into the dining room to see what the ruckus was all about. "Is it just me, or is this very obscure and random?"

Grandma tapped her chin thoughtfully. "The Partridge Family. A pear." She looked up with glee. "A Partridge in a pear tree!"

Mandy shook her head. "How funny is that? I mean, why me?"

"What's today?" Grandma was going for the calendar, and counting the squares. "Today's the fourteenth. It's twelve days to Christmas."

Grandpa made his way back to his recliner, shaking his head and mumbling. "Christmas starts earlier every year."

CLAY WAS CHOMPING at the bit to know how his gifts were being received. He'd used various means to get the gifts to her, and early reports were favorable.

When a thought came to him, he grabbed his phone, pulled up his messaging app, and plugged in Caryn's contact info.

> OTDMR

Caryn texted him back immediately.

> What on earth?

> You wanted a name for our operation.
> Operation Twelve Days of Mandy Reno.

Caryn sent him a string of laughing emojis ending with a big red heart.

He'd left his "two turtle doves" offering of a bracelet with two doves on the counter of the Clementville Café when no one was looking, and at church today, she was wearing it. He smiled as he drove down the road to his grandparents' house. He'd been determined to take care of that one himself.

He was forced to include a few more people in his deception than he wanted, but so far, everyone had been more than happy to be in on the plan. Ben was surprisingly encouraging. He'd expected ragging after the initial surprise at Clay's choice, but it seemed his friend was growing up. He'd been more thoughtful lately, less loose-cannon and more steady-Eddie. Caryn probably had something to do with that, because Ben was becoming positively domesticated.

The French cookbook was sent directly to her in the mail, gift-wrapped. That took care of "three French hens." He hoped someday he'd get to taste a few of the recipes. That was probably stretching it.

The only thing he could find for "four calling birds" was a phone case with four flamingos on it. He'd had Darcy, Roxy's daughter, give it to Mandy when she came in to work that afternoon.

On Friday, for "five golden rings," Clay dropped five huge Amish-made donuts on the doorstep of the RenoVations Inc., office. He'd had to let Lisa in on it because he wasn't completely sure that squirrels, groundhogs, or dogs wouldn't help themselves. And to pay for her silence, he had to give up the sixth donut in the half-dozen he'd bought. It was worth it.

Acquiring six large, golden, fillable plastic eggs would have been difficult this time of year if not for the beauty of the Internet. At least he didn't have to worry about the candy inside melting this time of year. These he left on the front porch of her grandparents' house when he knew Mandy wouldn't be there. Caryn had distracted her with a shopping trip, but her grandmother, Sylvia Reno, caught him red-handed, not as surprised as he would have thought.

She, too, was sworn to secrecy.

Would all these people be able to keep the secret? Today he'd gone to church very early and left her "seven swans a-swimming" gift—a musical picture book of Swan Lake—in their Bible Study room. The only people there that early were the pastor, Brother Aaron, and Shawn, the youth minister. They would make good cops—he didn't have a chance to get away with it before they caught him. They saw him come in with the gift, so he had to tell them.

So far, upon discovery, everyone had seemed surprised but pleased that he was doing this. Was it such a stretch? Was he so predictable?

He drew his brows together in a frown. Had he played it safe all these years? Not professionally. He'd gotten his degree in criminal justice, then a short stint as a police officer in Bowling Green before running for sheriff. That was a fluke, he thought. The incumbent sheriff wanted to retire, so he didn't have anyone running against him, and he was ready to come home. Winning his second election felt like more of a victory.

But as far as relationships, after he and Lisa parted as friends but nothing more, he'd let that part of his life take a back seat to the job. It was easier to simply shut himself off. Between taking care of an entire county and seeing after his mom and grandparents, he hadn't thought much about relationships until recently. Maybe he was in a groove with the job. Maybe things had eased up with his family.

Or maybe until he realized that Mandy Reno wasn't the middle-school kid with a ponytail who had been Lisa's shadow growing up.

She could certainly sport a ponytail these days, but gone was the gangling teenager he'd remembered before she came back home in the summer. She was beautiful. While she was in college at Murray State, she was home in the summer, but she was a busy girl. When she started working part-time at the café last May, he'd seen her regularly, and the more he got to know her, the more he found himself looking for her.

He wasn't stalking her, was he? As an officer of the law, he didn't want her to think he was a creep. So far, all reports had been that she was pleased with the gifts, and he was on the home stretch. Five more days of gifts, five more days of keeping the secret. There was a part of him that wanted her to figure it out.

His greatest fear was that he would reveal his secret and see a sudden look of horror cross her face.

That reaction would be devastating, but he had to prepare for the possibility.

Chapter 6

December 22

Mandy worked her luxurious dark hair into a French braid to get ready for work at the café. She'd pulled lunch duty, and she had to admit to a slight case of jitters. Or was it anticipation?

What would she find today?

Three weeks ago, she was devastated to think she would have Christmas without her parents, but now she was a little overwhelmed by the attention given to her by gifts bestowed upon her by the person she'd decided, as a joke, to call "The Christmas Stalker." She didn't think it was a stalker, really, but as excited as she got every day when she came across a new gift from her secret admirer, she outwardly tried to downplay it.

She'd taken to looking at every customer at the café and everyone at church as a potential Secret Santa. The gift-giver could be male or female. It wasn't as if the gifts were romantic, and it could be a well-meaning sister in Christ who knew Mandy needed a pick-me-up.

But the bracelet. That was different. It spoke to her.

It was so pretty. Fingering the fine silver chain with two delicate doves connected by a single heart, Mandy realized when she put it on to go to church on Sunday, that she'd worn it every day since it arrived. Who knew she was a bracelet girl?

The aggravating but thrilling part of the whole thing was that it seemed everyone knew who her benefactor was except her. She'd figure it out, hopefully, before Christmas, which was this Friday. She had no idea what was in store for her this week. If it stopped, she would be disappointed.

She picked up the card that was included with the bracelet. Five capital letters: OTDMR in block letters, no other signature.

What could those letters stand for?

Hmm. *Old Tactical Dreamy Magical Romantic?*

Overly Tricky Distributor of Merry Remembrance?

She'd tried different word combinations, but absolutely none of them made sense.

Mandy held up her arm and admired the bracelet one more time in the mirror, and popped a Milkmaids Caramel candy in her mouth that she'd found in the mailbox. Eight maids a-milking.

"What's so funny?"

Grandma was passing her room and stuck her head in to see her youngest granddaughter admiring her gifts.

"It's just so weird that this is happening to me."

"What's weird about it?" Grandma's eyes sparkled with the secret. She loved her grandmother, but these last few weeks she had seen the side of Grandma that her children had seen when they were kids. The anticipation of the holiday. The love of surprise. The love of family. Her benefactor not only helped Mandy but also brought a spark to her grandparents. They were as excited to see each day's gift as she was.

Mandy walked over to Grandma and hugged her. "I don't

know whether to think someone has a crush on me or if some well-meaning friend is just trying to cheer me up."

"I see." When Grandma's eyebrow lifted, Mandy knew that *she* knew the identity of her gift-giver.

"You know who it is." In her prime spot in the family as the youngest grandchild, she was fairly certain she could wheedle it out of Grandma eventually. But after noting the look in Grandma's eye, Mandy was less certain of that fact.

"I do, but I've been sworn to secrecy. Have you ever known me to break a promise?"

"No, I haven't." Mandy felt her eyebrow raise in imitation of her grandmother. She'd been told that she was the "spitting image" of Sylvia Reno in her younger days, and she was beginning to see it more and more as she spent this extended time with her. "But it's not worrying you, so I can assume that my Christmas Stalker isn't in the real stalker category?"

"Oh my, no." Grandma looked at her watch. "Would you look at the time? Someone is going to be late for work if she doesn't skedaddle."

"I just wonder what will arrive for 'nine ladies dancing.'"

"You'll just have to wait and see, young lady." She gave her granddaughter another hug and whispered in her ear. "Don't spoil the surprise. I have a feeling it may be one of the best you've ever had."

THE EXTREMELY LIGHT gift bag was hanging on a hook in the coat room of the café, next to the back door, where she hung her coat and scarf when she got to work. *So, this person, whomever it is that Grandma approves of, has access to the kitchen.*

Who am I kidding?

It's Clementville. It could be anybody.

"Oh. Mandy. You just about scared me to death. I didn't hear you come in." Roxy had a hand to her chest and was looking around her nervously.

"Just did." She held up the gift bag and shook it a little. "I don't think this bag will hold 'nine ladies dancing,' do you?" Mandy laughed as her boss reddened slightly and shook her head.

"You have no idea, do you?" Roxy let out a frustrated sigh.

"No, and I keep finding out that more and more people know who it is, and they're not telling me." She shook her head and pulled out tissue paper to find a squarish object wrapped in white glittery paper. "And now they're wrapping in layers."

"What is it?"

Mandy ripped the paper and smiled happily. "Yay! It's a DVD of *White Christmas!*" She looked up at Roxy. "How did they know that it's my favorite Christmas movie?"

"I'll bet at least nine ladies are dancing in one of those scenes."

She nodded, her face flushing with pleasure. How did her benefactor know so much about her? She looked at Roxy closely. How could she frame this question? "Please tell me this isn't a relative?"

Roxy's face crumbled in laughter. "Girl, you will be so surprised." She looked behind her to see if anyone was listening. "You didn't hear it from me, but I can tell you one thing—it's not a relative."

A chilling thought came to her. Could it be Thomas? That took some of the joy out of the whole thing, but she wouldn't think about that now ...

Hmm. Maybe I am Scarlett O'Hara.

"Thank the Lord." Mandy closed her eyes in relief. "But it still might be someone just trying to cheer me up."

"Maybe it is." The older woman smiled gently. "And that's what friends are for, isn't it?"

That fluttery feeling in her stomach settled down a bit. Maybe it was a well-meaning friend. There was only one thing she could do. Wait, and hope that the person behind this eventually reveals him or herself.

She looked down at her wrist at her favorite gift so far, enjoying the sparkle. The bracelet. Was she destined to be disappointed by attaching romantic notions to the delicate piece of jewelry?

If it's Thomas, I may swear off dating for life.

Chapter 7

"I'll be there in ten."

Clay ended the call abruptly. The hospital called just after his grandmother had tried to call him. He'd been on a call in an area without cell service, and once he returned to town, his phone blew up with messages.

Mom had been taken to the hospital, unconscious, around 10 a.m. He checked the time—10:30.

He turned on his siren and flew through the stoplight between the courthouse and the hospital. Besides his grandparents, Mom was all he had left. What would he do if she ... No, he wouldn't think in those terms.

Are you there, God? Mom needs you. I don't know what's going on, but I know You do ...

He barely remembered removing his keys from the ignition and rushing through the automatic doors of the hospital's Emergency Room entrance.

"Clay, she's in room three." The nurse in scrubs held the security door open for him.

He never stopped until he entered the room where Mom

"

lay, so still and pale. There were electrodes and an IV hooked up to her. He looked at Sandra, the nurse recording her vital signs. "What's going on?"

"We got a 9-1-1 call from your grandmother that your mom had collapsed and they couldn't rouse her. She's been in and out of consciousness since she arrived, and we're running a series of tests to see what's happening." Sandra leveled him with a glance. "Has she shown any signs of depression or anxiety? Panic attacks?"

Clay raked his hand over his face. "All of the above."

She nodded. "I thought so." Sandra perked up when she heard other voices. "I think your grandparents are here."

"I'll talk to them and see if they'll wait in the lobby." He shook his head. "Grandma may want to come back here."

"That's fine. They can both come in, but only one needs to stay with her. We're limited on space." She reset the vital signs monitor. "Her heart rate is good, Clay. The doctor is reading some other tests, and he'll be in as soon as he knows anything." She squeezed his shoulder and smiled, leaving silently.

Clay took a deep breath, then closed his eyes briefly. He knew what day it was.

December 22. Ten years ago, today. The day a senseless accident robbed them of a husband and a father. It was always bad, the closer it got to Christmas. But this year? What was it about an anniversary of a tragedy that pulled it all out and displayed it in front of everything, minimizing the positive, and flaunting the horror of the event?

Probably why we've never done a lot of celebrating at Christmas.

He took his mom's hand and looked at the blue veins on the back. It was a small hand. It was up to him to take care of her. It was why he became County Sheriff, so he could be closer to home. He'd fallen down on the job. Dreaming of a life of his own felt like the height of selfishness. This crazy thing he started for Mandy? In the light of his mother lying on a gurney in the ER, it felt juvenile.

Rubbing the top of her hand and then laying it down carefully, he made his way back to the hallway where his grandparents, Mom's parents, waited.

Granny had been crying, and Granddad had his arm around his wife of nearly sixty years.

"Hey."

Granny went right to him. "Are you all right, sweetheart?"

He had to smile. She wanted to take care of him, and he was twice her size, if not more.

"I'm okay. Her vitals are looking better."

"Can I see Diane?"

"Yeah, Sandra's on duty, and she said you could go back there for a few minutes." Clay gave her a brief smile. "She's in and out of consciousness."

"I don't know what happened. We had breakfast, and she went to take a shower. We were going to run to the dollar store to pick up a few things. When she took too long and I didn't hear water running, I went in, and there she was, dressed, laying on the floor." Granny shook her head. "I've been worried about her."

"Yeah, me too." Clay glanced at Granddad, who nodded quietly. They all knew what day it was.

Clay pulled back the curtain to admit his grandparents into the ER cubicle, glad to see Mom's eyes open.

"Clay." Mom turned her head toward him and reached out her hand, her gaze confused and a little wild. "I'm so sorry."

Always with the apologies, when it was he that should have done more.

"For what, Mom?" He pulled the rolling stool up next to her, putting himself at eye level instead of towering over her.

Granny and Granddad went to the other side of the gurney. "Mom, Dad, you didn't need to come up here."

Granddad blew his nose on the handkerchief he kept in his pants pocket, and Granny smoothed back Mom's hair as she would have done when she was a little girl. "No way we could stay home and not know what was going on."

Mom closed her eyes, tears leaking out from beneath her lashes. "Oh, Mom. I didn't mean to."

Doctor Boyd came in with a chart, startled to see so many in the alcove. "I see we're all here." He smiled. "We don't have a lot of room, but you're the only patient back here at the moment." He shook Clay's hand. "Sheriff."

"What's going on, Doc?"

The doctor looked down at the papers in his hand, then at Mom. "Do you want to tell them, or shall I?"

IF HIS GRANDPARENTS hadn't found Mom when they did, she might have died.

After talking to Mom and getting her to rest, his grandparents went home. He had to get out of there. Sitting in the Jeep, he had a sour taste in his mouth. The taste of dread. When the doctor explained what her depression had the potential to do, his heart almost stopped.

It was something he had feared for so long but kept pushing down the fear that she would try to hurt herself.

She promised him that she just wanted to sleep away the day and took an extra over-the-counter sleeping pill. She didn't think it would affect her seriously. A good long nap. That's all she wanted.

So she said. She insisted—begged them to believe her.

Could he? Could he trust her anymore?

He'd noticed the weight loss over the last year. She was frail and looked much older than her fifty-three years. She and Grandma could pass for sisters.

Closing his eyes, he let it go. Tears ran down his face. Had he cried when Dad died? He couldn't remember. All he could pull up from that time was anger that his alcoholic father had been killed in a car accident, and it had nothing to do with alcohol. He'd been on the verge of getting clean for the first time in years when he died.

So close.

It wasn't fair.

But Mom. She'd never been the same. She'd cried enough tears for herself and him, too, he guessed.

A fleeting thought of Mandy and the gifts he'd arranged clamored into his mind. He was so close to Christmas, and he had it all arranged. He'd have to get Ben to make sure it all happened.

At this point, he had nothing to offer Mandy except his friendship. The idea of saddling anyone with this situation made him sick. It wasn't going to happen, couldn't happen, even if it took every ounce of control he had.

The peck on the window next to his head made him want to jump out of his skin. Seeing the doctor there, he almost wanted to put the Jeep in reverse and just drive. Drive until he couldn't drive anymore.

Instead, he raked a hand over his face and got out of the vehicle.

"You okay?" Doc looked as concerned for him as for Mom.

"I'm fine. Is Mom okay?"

Doc Boyd took a deep breath, then exhaled. "She's stable, physically, but I'm worried about her state of mind."

"What can I do to help?"

The doctor gave him a half-smile and shook his head. "You can't fix everything, Clay, even if you are the sheriff." He put a hand on Clay's shoulder and squeezed.

Clay looked away, staring up at the sky, trying to get hold of himself. He whispered. "What can I say to her, Doc?"

"That you love her, and you're there for her."

An abrupt nod was all Clay could produce. Was this going to hang over him for the rest of their lives? The part of him that felt guilty for not lavishing her with attention was at war with the part of him that was angry. Angry at Dad for getting himself killed, and angry at Mom for taking such drastic steps. Angry that as much as he tried to follow God's will, things like this still happened.

"Don't shy away from it, Clay. She's saying she didn't take the pills trying to die, and I believe her." Doc cleared his throat of the emotion Clay could hear in his voice. "Sometimes it's not about ending a life, but about ending pain. Pain that for some reason your mom can't fathom lessening."

"Thanks, Doc."

"Any time." Doc tilted his head to make Clay look him in the eye. "I'm here for you too. You have a life to live."

Clay scoffed. "Some life."

"She's made her choices, and you have to decide if you're going to let those choices color yours." Doc paused. "I think she may need to be admitted to a hospital for a few days."

Clay's jaw set. "Are you saying she's crazy, Doc? That she needs to go to Western State Hospital?" That had been a fear for a long time. Now it was voiced.

"No, she's not crazy, and I'm not suggesting Western. There are some good facilities out there that serve the whole body. She's not healthy physically *or* mentally. Did you know she weighs less than a hundred pounds?"

"I knew she'd lost weight."

"And I'm concerned about the results of her bloodwork. Low on everything you can think of that you need in your blood. If she's in the hospital, we can treat the body and the mind at the same time, and maybe help her get through this more quickly."

What could he say to that? It made sense, and he couldn't put off the inevitable conversation.

"I'll talk to her."

Chapter 8

December 23

"A jump rope?" Mandy held the gift up, puzzled. She'd found the gift bag hanging on the back door of her grandparents' house first thing that morning, and couldn't wait to see what it was. She had to say, whoever was treating her to the ongoing stream of gifts was original, because there didn't seem to be any rhyme or reason to the sequence of events except for the number.

"Ten lords a-leaping." Grandpa chuckled. "I guess your mystery date expects you to do the leaping this time."

"Very funny." She looked at him sideways. "And who says it's a mystery date?"

Grandpa raised his eyebrows and chuckled. "If it's not, you're going to be awful disappointed, aren't you?" He winked at her and made his way to the coffee pot.

So, Grandpa knew who it was too. Was the whole community conspiring against her? Or would that be *for* her?

CLAY DIDN'T FORGET the tenth day of Christmas, but it was touch and go accomplishing it. Ben said Mandy nearly caught him sneaking up to the back door of the elder Reno's house. Some trick to accomplish without dogs and chickens giving him away.

The doctor wanted to keep an eye on Mom overnight, then transfer her to a facility in Madisonville, so he was heading to Marion to pick her up. She finally got up the nerve to tell them what happened.

She'd taken her anti-anxiety medication as usual, but when she was in the shower, she had a panic attack thinking about what the day meant. Ten years since Dad was killed. The shock had thrown her into a state of trauma that flared up without warning.

Ten long years.

When she calmed down enough to get out and get dressed, she saw some PM medication on the counter, and, since the anxiety pill hadn't seemed to help and she hadn't slept well the night before, she took one of those. Maybe sleep would help. She kept saying she hadn't tried to kill herself. She just wanted the pain gone. What she didn't know was that that particular combination of drugs taken so close together, could have been lethal.

Why, Mom?

Pulling into the parking lot of the hospital, he sat in the car for a few minutes, thinking. Praying, then continuing to pray as he strode down the hallway of the small hospital.

God, give Mom the gift of peace. Please. Is there anything I can do?

When he arrived at her room, she was sitting up, dressed,

waiting for him. "Mornin', sweetheart." She patted the bed beside her, and he sat next to her.

"How are you feeling this morning?" Clay searched her face, looking for some signal of what she was feeling and thinking.

"Better. Tired." She tried to smile as she took his big hand in her own and looked down at it. "Can you ever forgive me?" The tears in her eyes were almost more than he could take.

"Of course, I can, Mom." He shook his head incredulously. "We're in this together, you and me."

She nodded. "You've spent the last ten years taking care of me when you should be making a life for yourself."

"I'm doing okay, Mom."

She pursed her lips. "Clay, I had a little bit of a breakthrough last night. It may not last the rest of the day, but yesterday, when I was on that gurney in the ER, all of you standing there, worried about me, there was a point where I wanted to die. It would be better for everyone if I weren't here."

Chapter 9

December 24

Coming back into town from taking Mom to Madisonville, Clay opened the door of the café. Lunch happened whether he felt like eating or not.

The happy sound of the jingle bells felt out of place as they gave out their holiday cheer.

Mandy strode across the dining room with a smile. Quite a change from a few weeks ago when he could hardly coax a grin from her, and now he had a hard time smiling himself. Then he saw the bracelet on her wrist sparkle in the light, lifting his spirits.

Thank you, God.

"Hey, Clay. How are you?"

"I'm okay."

"How's your mom?" The compassion in her eyes reached into his soul.

"She's going to be in the hospital in Madisonville for a few days." He looked down, unable to meet her eyes. If his mother's mental illness was hereditary, maybe that's why God hadn't seen fit to give him a wife and family yet.

"I hope she can get the help she needs."

Clay nodded. Time for a change of subject. He still had few surprises left. He'd finish the job even if he couldn't promise her more than friendship. That would have to be enough. He glanced up, noting the wistful expression on her face. He needed to buck up.

"Are you going to the Christmas Eve service?"

"I'm going with Grandma and Grandpa. It's cool that the area churches take turns hosting the service, isn't it?" Mandy grabbed a set of silverware and a menu. "Where would you like to sit? Table or booth?"

There weren't many people there for lunch today. It was Christmas Eve, after all. "A booth might be nice."

"A booth it is. Looks like you could have your pick."

"I'll let you choose." He quirked an eyebrow at her, wishing he had the nerve to ask her to join him.

"All right. How about this lovely setup here?" She gestured in her best Vanna White imitation to the second booth from the back.

Clay chuckled. It felt good. "Perfect. I knew you would choose well." He took the menu and pretended to peruse it closely. "You're chipper today."

"It's Christmas Eve, and we're closing early so we can celebrate. Darcy's off to Atlanta to take the twins to see their other grandparents, so I told Roxy I'd be glad to fill in. I don't have kids to worry about. Tonight's the extended Reno Christmas at Grandma's."

"The whole clan, huh?"

"Nearly. We're missing a few besides Mom and Dad. Grandma's running around like a chicken with her head cut off

—but she's having a ball." She lifted a shoulder. "But enough about me. What can I get you to drink?"

"How about some of that 'House of Grace' tea?"

The special non-alcoholic concoction was only available during the Christmas holidays, and the drink, created first at a restaurant in Paducah, was a mixture of sweetened tea, white grape juice, and other ingredients. Not everyone liked it, but it seemed Christmas-y to him, today.

"Coming right up." She glanced at him. "Would you like a gallon to go? Roxy has about three in the cooler that will go to waste since we're closing early." She grinned. "I don't anticipate a rush."

"Good idea. I'll be glad to take some off your hands." He would take some to Mom this afternoon.

She turned to go, and Clay stopped her with his words. "Mandy ..."

Pausing, she turned back, eyebrows raised, lips quirked in a half-smile.

When she looked at him like that, he nearly lost his train of thought. "I'm glad you're feeling better."

A slow smile graced her lips. "Thanks, Clay. I appreciate it. It seems like the whole community has worked hard to make this a good Christmas for me."

"I understand there's a mystery going on concerning gifts showing up at odd times." He narrowed his gaze on her, trying to look as serious as possible. "You want me to look into it?"

She laughed. "No, I'm trying to be patient. The only clue I've been able to get out of anyone is that it's not a relative." She shrugged her shoulders and rushed off to get his drink.

He was so glad this was nearly over because if it went much further, she would figure it out for sure. Roxy waved at him from the kitchen and had a sheepish look on her face when she shrugged, holding out her hands. He simply waved and shook his head. So, Roxy was the weak link? He was surprised he hadn't given it away himself.

When Mandy came back, she paused to talk, since there were only three other customers in the place. "I'm not sure what will happen today. I haven't gotten anything yet, and I can't imagine what gift would represent 'eleven pipers piping.'"

"It's a mystery all right." He held the menu up, afraid she would read it all over his face. "If you get worried about it, I'd be glad to get some extra deputies on deck to find out who this joker is."

She narrowed her eyes a bit. "You know, too, don't you?"

For the first time in a couple of days, he felt his lips curve in a smile. Mandy reddened, then rolled her eyes and swept away with a decided *humph* that made him want to laugh.

That inclination ended when the door jingled again and he saw Mandy stop in her tracks. It was that guy who was there the night all of this started.

Old boyfriend? Current boyfriend?

Didn't matter.

Once this gift-giving spate was done, he would try to distance himself from the girl who could've meant the world to him.

He had a feeling everything would taste like sawdust for the rest of the holiday.

Chapter 10

Mandy turned when the door jingled, feeling her stomach drop to her feet.

Thomas. What was he doing here?

Looking around, there was nobody else to whom she could foist the unwelcome guest. And she didn't have the right to discourage Roxy's business.

She took a deep breath and walked right up to him. "Welcome to Clementville Café. Where would you like to sit?"

Thomas hadn't said a word—she hadn't given him a chance, yet.

"Booth is fine." He looked around at the nearly empty dining room.

She saw his eyebrows raise, and a look of fear come across his features as his eyes rested on Clay, in uniform, sidearm visible.

Probably noticing that I have friends in high places.

"Mandy, I ..."

"Here you go." She waved him into the booth and set a

placemat and silverware in front of him. "Would you like to order your drink?"

"Um ... sure." He looked at the menu.

"I recommend the House of Grace Tea if you're in a festive mood." Could her jaw clench any tighter?

"I couldn't get up the nerve to talk to you last time I was here, but I wanted to tell you I'm sorry, Mandy."

She finally met his eyes. Maybe her stare would bore a hole into him, and he'd leave and be gone forever, walking around the world with a stare-sized negative space in the region of his heart.

He repeated it. "I'm sorry, Mandy."

"Thomas, I told you in August it was over between us. I can't handle being around someone I should be afraid of every time he gets upset." She wanted to growl but settled for a huff instead. "If you keep showing up where I work, I will file a restraining order."

"And that's exactly why I'm here." Thomas's eyes cut in the direction of Clay. "I've ... I've been going through a twelve-step program for anger management."

"Anger management?"

He nodded then looked down for a second. "Step eight is making amends to anyone I've hurt, and that's why I'm here."

It made so much sense. The way he'd seemed to dismiss what she wanted to do and talk her into going along with him. He'd had her almost believing he was smarter and more rational than she, and she finally had enough. She'd suspected him of drinking, but their last date had ended with an argument when he wanted to proceed with their relationship more quickly than she was ready. When he'd reared back to hit her, that was it.

Mandy slid into the booth across from him. "So, that's why ..."

"That's why I tried to control everything about our relationship. I thought if I could talk you into going along with me, it would make me happy, and then you would be happy. I was a little tipsy the last time we talked." He shook his head. "How stupid can a guy get?"

She arched a brow. "Tipsy? You were drunk, and it wasn't the first time. If I told you everything I thought about you since then, you'd tuck your tail between your legs and shake off the dust of Clementville forever."

He relaxed, chuckling softly. "I get it."

"And I'm not even apologizing for mixing my metaphors."

"No apology needed. I understand."

"But I did mean what I said in August—about not seeing each other anymore." Mandy looked up when Clay passed her to pay his bill. His eyes met hers and she gave him a slight nod, answering him with a small smile.

"I accept that." He reached his hand across the table. "Friends?"

She narrowed her eyes. "With absolutely no benefits other than my forgiveness?"

He nodded.

"Then friends, it is. We both live in the same part of the state. It's a small region. We're bound to run into one another eventually."

Roxy stepped up to the cash register to check Clay out. She'd wanted to do that.

Thomas looked in the direction she was. "The sheriff?"

Heat rolled over her face. "He's a good friend."

Thomas nodded. "Looks like a nice guy." He cleared his throat. "Another thing I wanted to share with you is that through the recovery program, I became a believer." It was as if he were afraid to tell her. "I knew that was important to you."

"You didn't ..." Mandy sputtered.

His lips spread in a half-smile. "No, I didn't come to Jesus to get closer to you."

"That's a relief."

"Funny, though, when we were dating, it irked me to think you put God ahead of me." He shook his head. "Now I get it. Crazy, huh?"

"Oh, Thomas." She was so surprised that she impulsively reached out and took his hand. "You've made my day. Giving your life to Jesus? That's the best recovery you can have. Talk about a support system. I mean, Jesus, right? Perfect."

Chapter 11

December 24, evening

Mandy was stuffed.

Grandma had hosted their regular whole-family get-together with her brother and sister and families, Uncle Steve and his family.

The only ones missing were Mom and Dad, Uncle Tom, Aunt Ginger, and their family. It was always a treat when the *away* cousins came for a visit from Alabama. Now that they were all adults, like Mandy, it was harder to get schedules together.

Next year. They promised. She refused to believe they would go another Christmas without everyone coming together at Grandma and Grandpa's house.

Pork roast with all the fixings and four kinds of pie was greatly appreciated, and their "Dirty Santa" game with aunts, uncles, cousins, and nieces and nephews was hilarious. Somehow, she ended up with a gallon of windshield-wiper fluid, mainly because her cousin Del had it, and she had to steal it from him. It had nothing to do with the *what,* but the *who* in this game.

The candlelit church was peaceful after the madness, and it would have been so easy to fall asleep. She sat on the end of the pew of the fairly crowded sanctuary, next to her grandparents. Her brother and sister and their families were in the pew in front, and Uncle Steve's family sat behind them. She looked around, waving quietly at this one or that, catching Caryn's eye and sending a smile her way as she sat halfway back with her boyfriend Ben. The music was just beginning, and the pipe organ was amazing.

Just before the service began, someone tapped her shoulder. "Is anyone sitting here?" It was Clay, looking unsure of himself.

A little flummoxed, Mandy smiled up at him, wondering if she was blushing "It's a free church." Wow. She had that come-hither line down, didn't she? Was her face radiating heat? Would anyone notice if she just slid under the pew now?

She scooted down, making room for him.

"Thanks, I thought maybe your boyfriend was coming ..."

Boyfriend?

She frowned, about to speak, but Clay kept talking.

"My grandparents have been through a lot this week and didn't feel like coming out tonight, but I wanted to be here."

"I'm glad you came." Maybe she misheard. Then it hit her.

He'd seen her with Thomas this afternoon.

Should she tell him she didn't have a boyfriend, or simply leave it alone? Did it bother him, the thought of her having a boyfriend? *Hmm ...*

"Me too. Have I missed anything?"

"Just me nearly falling asleep from the huge meal we just finished. Grandma pulled out all the stops tonight, and we'll do it all over again tomorrow."

He patted his stomach. "I know how you feel. Gram just cooked for the three of us with Mom in the hospital, but there may as well have been an army regiment there to eat it." He smiled down at her. "Remember when we were kids, and we were so anxious for Santa to come that we couldn't eat or sleep?"

"Yes. At Grandma Reno's, we couldn't open presents until the dishes were washed. Is that not child abuse?" She chuckled. "When did everything change?"

Clay shook his head and sighed. "About the time we became teenagers, I'm guessing."

Mandy covered her mouth to keep from laughing, glancing up at the platform, and then back at Clay. "For me, it was when I found my Christmas presents in the hall closet."

"Ouch. Were you looking?"

She gave him a flat look. "I was ten. Of course, I was looking."

He laughed. "I was nine. New sled in the barn." He raised his eyebrows in question.

"Barbie for President doll."

"Seriously?"

When she nodded, he looked at her incredulously, then as her smile broke out, he laughed out loud.

Grandma leaned over to shush them when their chuckle and giggle threatened to be heard outside their pew. "They're getting ready to start, you two."

"Yes, ma'am." Mandy sat up a little straighter, but she shot a glance at Clay, who was about as red-faced as she'd seen him.

I did that.

She wriggled in her seat, somehow pleased at the idea.

THE LIGHTS DIMMED as the pianist and organist took their places. It was a simple service, no bells and whistles.

A hush came over the congregation as the choir entered from each side of the sanctuary, quietly singing "Away in a Manger." The children in makeshift costumes taking their places as they portrayed the nativity brought back memories of Christmas past.

Clay remembered one year playing the part of a shepherd as Mandy, with her dark hair and sweet countenance, played the part of Mary.

Mary, who was favored above all women.

Where that came from, he wasn't sure, but he pondered it.

Clay looked down at Mandy's upturned face. *What is it about Christmas? Even when we get caught up with festivities and forget that it's not about us—it's made better for the reminder of the Christ Child. The child who became the sacrifice for our sins.*

Passages in the second chapter of Luke were read and recited, songs were sung, and the finale was coming up. He was getting nervous, his attention warring between worshiping his Savior and attraction to a girl. Who did he think he was, anyway, asking the pastor of a church—not his own—to be a part of his deception? The minister probably thought he was crazy, sacrilegious, or both.

There was a slight pause, and the back doors opened letting in a swirl of cold air. The crowd, almost as one, turned to see what was happening. Suddenly, beautiful music soared from an ensemble of flutists walking up the aisle in single file, playing in perfect harmony, "Still, Still, Still." The congregation gasped in delight. When Clay cut his eyes at Mandy, he was happy to see that she was enthralled, as well. His heart was pumping hard, but the look on her face gave him all the confidence he needed for this, the next-to-last gift in the series.

"Clay." She reached over and grabbed his arm, squeezing it

almost painfully as she kept her eyes on the group standing on the steps of the platform.

He covered her hand with his and looked down, trying his best to keep a straight face in light of her sagging jaw.

Mandy whispered loudly, in awe. "There are eleven of them."

"Eleven what?"

She gazed up at him, her eyes round with joy and wonder, and shimmering with tears. "Eleven pipers piping."

Chapter 12

December 25

"Y ou're up awfully early."

Mandy had already made a pot of coffee and had hoped to beat her grandmother to mixing up a breakfast casserole. The butterscotch pull-aparts were rising on top of the range, where they'd been all night, and somehow, she couldn't keep the smile off her face.

"You worked hard yesterday, so I thought I'd get a head start for you today." She handed Grandma a cup of steaming hot coffee.

"I won't argue with that." She took a sip and looked closely at her youngest granddaughter. "Last night was nice, wasn't it?"

Mandy turned and tried to keep her eyes on the recipe card, but when Grandma didn't say anything else, she looked up, knowing her face was flushed. "It was." She cracked a dozen eggs in the bowl and pulled the whisk out of the drawer. "I still can't get over 'eleven pipers piping.'"

Grandma laughed out loud. "Me, either." She shot an eyebrow up. "I just wonder who is behind all this?"

"Like you don't know." Mandy thought a minute, pausing the whisk. "I have a few ideas, but every time I think I have it figured out, the next gift comes, and it's totally random."

"Maybe it's more than one person."

"Could be, but I don't think so. Random presents, but well-organized in execution. It's been too smooth. Like a well-oiled machine." She frowned for a minute. "Whoever it is, they got my mind off of Mom and Dad not being here."

"Maybe that was the idea."

She smiled, a wistful look on her face. "It's been nice. In a way, I'm glad I don't know." She shot her grandmother a look. "But now that it's Christmas Day, I want to find out."

"Something tells me that whoever is behind this won't reveal themselves immediately. They'll make you work for it."

"It was nice of you to invite Clay." She cut her eyes at her grandmother, curious. She had her suspicions but was afraid to hope. "You didn't have to. It's not like we're dating or anything."

Grandma shrugged. "I know. I just thought, since we're down two, that we would include him since he doesn't have much family, and his mama's in the hospital."

"It was nice." That's all she would say. Was Grandma doing a little match-making?

CLAY PULLED the red sweater over his head and looked at himself in the mirror. He didn't have much opportunity to wear civvies, so he felt a little self-conscious. The invitation to the Reno Christmas celebration was unexpected, but the glint in Sylvia Reno's eye was all the encouragement he needed to accept. He wasn't pinning his hopes on it. He had the image of Mandy throwing her arms around the neck of the dark-haired guy at the café, and that stifled most of the hope he'd begun to have for any more than friendship. It was better this way. That guy looked closer to her age too.

He caught a glimpse of himself in the mirror, and then his eyes fell on a Christmas card he'd received from Mandy's grandparents.

*Every good gift and every perfect gift is from above, and cometh down from the Father of lights, with whom is no variableness, neither shadow of turning.—*James 1:17

His gifts to Mandy were paltry representations of what God had given to the world if only the world would see it. And what about himself? What gifts had he looked for? Before now, he had desired to help his community be the best it could be. Make sure his mother and grandparents were well and taken care of. Serve in his church to the best of his ability.

For so long he had desired to be married, and have children, but God hadn't seen fit to gift him in that way.

And that was okay.

The verse said it all. What gifts he had been given had come from above, and had come because of the love of God for him. He closed his eyes for a moment and sent up a silent prayer.

Thank you, God, for what You've done, and what You will do. Thank you for the hope I have, because of what You have done in the past. I'm trusting You with this, Lord, and whatever the outcome, Your will be done.

This time he appraised himself thoroughly in the mirror. Freshly brushed hair, still slightly wet from the shower, trimmed beard, festive sweater over dark-wash jeans, and boots. He was presentable, and he meant what he told God. His will be done. He would ride this out to the end—whatever that turned out to be.

Chapter 13

After picking up the remnants of gift wrap and tissue paper from the living room floor, the "littles" were off in the den playing with their toys. Only baby Chloe remained, her youngest niece—so far—and daughter of her sister, Cassie. While they cleaned up, Grandpa settled into his recliner with the sleeping baby in his arms. "This is the life," he said as Chloe went to sleep, and he followed soon after.

"Leave him be." Grandma chuckled when Mandy went to grab his foot and wake him up. "He's better when he's not underfoot."

Mandy laughed. "True." He tended to hover over Grandma, making sure she didn't overdo, and it drove his love a little crazy sometimes.

"What time are Mom and Dad calling?" Cassie tied the trash bag up for disposal and looked at the clock.

"At two, our time. They're only two hours ahead."

"That's good. It's not like they're in Africa."

Mandy laughed. "Yeah, that's too much math for this family."

"You got that right." Mandy's brother Robert reached out to take the trash bags from his sisters. "That's why I married a math teacher."

"Somebody has to know how to add and subtract." Rob's wife Ella—great with child, as the Bible would describe her— was sitting, smoothing out viable pieces of tissue paper. In this family, gift bags and tissue paper were meant to be reused as much as possible, so after the gift exchange was over, the women called dibs on the bags they especially liked. There were a few that had made the trip back and forth several times.

"It was the least I could do." Ella laughed with the rest of the cleaning crew.

"What time is your date coming?" The voice of her grandfather, whom they all thought asleep, surprised them.

"I thought you were asleep."

"Just resting my eyes. For some reason, I always get sleepy between breakfast and lunch on Christmas Day." He cleared his throat and checked the sleeping baby in the crook of his arm. "Well?"

"Well, what?" Mandy thought maybe he would forget what he asked. No such luck.

Instead, he spoke a little louder. "What time is your date coming?"

"He's not my *date*, Grandpa. Just a good friend."

"Yeah, you two seemed pretty *friendly* at the Christmas Eve service. I saw Grandma have to shush you."

Her face was flaming, she knew. "Clay is coming any time now."

"Good. He's a nice young man. I think I approve."

Mandy rolled her eyes, knowing it was a teenager's move. "I'm so glad." Her voice dripped with sarcasm.

When her grandfather winked at her, she laughed. "Watch it, old man."

"Oh, I'm watchin', all right."

Robert came back in from taking the trash to the bin, carrying a large gift-wrapped box. "I found this on the back doorstep." He looked at the envelope. "Looks like the Christmas Bandit has struck again."

"It's the Christmas Stalker, not the Christmas Bandit." Mandy rushed to retrieve the package from her brother, then caught herself. "Not that he's a stalker *or* a bandit." She read her name, carefully written in longhand, on the envelope. It was the first gift that had more than her name on it.

When she opened it, her smile grew.

This is my wish for you:
Comfort on difficult days,
Smiles when sadness intrudes,
Rainbows to follow the clouds,
Laughter to kiss your lips,
Sunsets to warm your heart,
Hugs when spirits sag,
Beauty for your eyes to see,
Friendships to brighten your being,
Faith so that you can believe,
Confidence for when you doubt,
Courage to know yourself,
Patience to accept the truth,
Love to complete your life.

— Ralph Waldo Emerson

Merry Christmas from your mystery Santa
OTDMR

Her heart fluttered inside her chest and tears pricked at her eyelids. She didn't quite know why. It wasn't that it was a romantic sentiment, and yet, it was. She never knew that this —*this*—was what she dreamed of when she found "the one." She didn't even know who it was, and yet ...

"What does it say?" Grandma had been very patient as she read through it the third time.

"I'll let you read it later." At this point, she didn't need a gift. The card was enough. But it was Christmas, after all, and she had a gift sitting in front of her.

She pulled the gift toward her, almost hating to ruin the beautiful paper and ribbon. She had just begun to tug at the bow on top when the doorbell rang.

"That's Clay." She hesitated. "I'll get the door."

"No, I'll get it. You open the present." Rob shook his head and eased past her between the table and the counter.

CLAY CLEARED his throat as he followed Rob to the kitchen.

"Looks like Mr. Reno is enjoying his Christmas." He noted Mandy's grandpa was sound asleep with his great-granddaughter relaxed in his arms.

"That's the best sleep there is, right there, with a sleeping baby on you. You don't want to move, because you don't want to wake them up." He smiled at Clay. "But to tell the truth, you really just don't want to move because it's the best feeling in the world."

"I can only imagine."

Rob quirked an eyebrow at him. "Oh, you'll get there."

"We'll see."

Nearing the kitchen door, Rob whispered, "She's about to open the present."

Clay was hoping she would open it before he arrived.

Could he keep the secret? It all depended on how she reacted to the gift. It wasn't easy coming up with the twelfth gift. "Twelve drummers drumming" didn't speak to him, so he opted to finish it up differently.

"Hi, Clay." Mandy beamed up at him. "You're just in time."

"Is this the Christmas Stalker's doing?" He narrowed his eyelids. "I still wonder if I need to put you under surveillance."

"You're so funny." She held the card to her chest. "The card was perfect."

"What did it say?" He lifted his lips slightly, belying the beating of his heart.

She tilted her head and glanced away a moment before looking him in the eye, chin tilted up. "It's personal."

Grandma handed Mandy a pair of scissors. "If you're not going to break that ribbon, cut it. I need to get dinner started."

Mandy laughed and took the scissors. "It is almost too pretty to open."

"But you will, so let's get on with it." Cassie put her hands on her hips impatiently.

"Yes, ma'am."

He watched patiently as she carefully cut the ribbon and untaped the sides. Who knew she was one of *those* present openers?

Chapter 14

"Oh. My. Word." Mandy stood there, looking down into the box, unable to speak for a moment. "It's ... it's a snow globe." She lifted it out of the box carefully. "And not just any snow globe."

The bubble wrap and tissue paper were discarded, and she turned the piece on the table until she found the winding mechanism. When she carefully turned the pear-shaped key, the tune "The Twelve Days of Christmas" played, and the Christmas tree and all the other items around it moved. Every day of the familiar twelve days carol was represented by an ornament on the tree or an item under the tree.

"How did he know that I loved snow globes?"

Her sister Cassie piped up, a knowing look on her face as she quite deliberately looked squarely at Mandy. "Who said it was a *he*? I seem to remember someone mentioning that it might be a dear friend who simply wants to spread Christmas cheer."

Mandy stuck her tongue out at her sister but then turned her attention to the gift. She was almost as freaked out as she was excited about the gift. She'd loved snow globes all her life, since her first plastic shake-up toy with fake plastic snow inside. This one required no shaking. The motor providing movement of the items inside also kept the snow swirling beautifully, a mixture of sparkle and white.

She sat at the table, gazing at it, counting all the items inside. "Look at this, y'all. On top is a partridge, and the key is a pear. There are the two turtle doves." She held up the bracelet on her wrist. It was still her favorite of all the gifts. "Three French hens, four calling birds." She held up her phone with the flamingo case and laughed.

Clay leaned over, looking at it closely. "There are the five golden rings, hanging on the tree." He laughed.

"I got five donuts for that one." She chuckled with him. "Six geese a laying—see? There they are on the tree."

"Seven swans, eight maids a milking. See the little milking stools?" The music slowed, so she had to turn the key again, this time a little more. "There are nine ballerinas and ten lords a leaping—they're frogs!"

He smiled when she met his eyes. "Where are the eleven pipers piping?"

"Here—eleven flutes, just like last night." She shook her head and sighed. "I'll never forget that. It was the best, wasn't it?"

"It was." He cleared his throat. "I think I count twelve drums."

"Yep, there are twelve." She sighed happily, tears poised on her lashes. "Oh, Clay, this is amazing, isn't it?"

"Somebody certainly thinks highly of you."

Mandy met his eyes and saw something there she hadn't noticed before. It wasn't as if she hadn't thought about it. She had, but with another semester of law school, did she want to start something she might have to let go? And if she started something, *could* she let go?

She looked away, using the snow globe as an excuse. "It's a little scary." Mandy realized that she had been left alone in the kitchen with Clay. "Where did everybody go?"

He looked around, seeming to be surprised, himself. "I didn't even notice when they left."

"I thought Grandma was all hyped up about starting dinner." She laughed and shook her head, then paused. Why would they leave her and Clay alone?

"WHY DID you say it was a little scary?" Clay looked deeply into her eyes every time he had a chance. She seemed to be avoiding just that situation, so when she did look his way, he had to be ready. Had to treat every opportunity as his last.

"Not, scary." Mandy looked thoughtful. "More like it's scary just how well whoever this is seems to know me. Am I so easy to read?"

He laughed out loud. "No, you are not."

"Good. I'd like to think there was some mystery about me." She huffed a little.

After a deep breath to settle his heartbeat, he sat down at the kitchen table across from where she had landed, reaching over to squeeze her hand. "I think there will always be a little mystery about you, Mandy."

With a quick nod and a smile, she seemed pleased. "Good. Lawyers have to have a little bit of a poker face, you know."

"I thought they just had to be good at arguing."

He let go of her hand when her brother came into the room. Rob shot a look at him and poured himself another cup of coffee, holding the pot up to see if anyone else wanted some. "She had the arguing part down by the time she was three years old." Apparently, he was going to pretend he saw nothing.

"Stop it, Rob."

"Just sayin'." Rob sat down at the table. "Any idea who this joker could be?" His coffee cup must have been awfully interesting because he stared at it like it was the most fascinating thing he'd ever seen.

"Not a clue." Mandy looked accusingly from one to the other. "Both of you know, don't you?"

She seemed a little outdone as the two men, classmates and teammates from way back, simply looked at one another and smiled.

Chapter 15

"I don't know what you wrote in that card, but it must have been good." Mandy's Grandma spoke quietly when they were out of earshot of the dining room. She'd signaled for Clay to join her in the kitchen. Taking the hint, he had offered to help her bring dessert out, and she seemed glad of his company. Probably so she could grill him.

"She didn't show you?" He was surprised.

Sylvia Reno shook her head and smirked at him. "She's keeping it close to the vest." She handed him two plates of pumpkin pie with fresh whipped cream, then crossed her arms in front of her. "So, young man, just what are your intentions toward my granddaughter?"

Saved by the phone. When his phone buzzed in his pocket, he pulled it out, seeing "Doc Boyd" on the caller-ID. He held up his finger to Mrs. Reno. "I need to take this."

She nodded her head. "Of course. I'll leave you alone."

Before he could stop her, she was out the door to give him privacy.

"Doc? What's goin' on?"

"Hey, Clay, just got a call from the hospital in Madisonville. Diane has had some kind of spell, and they need you down there."

"Why didn't they call me? They had my number?" He knew he was wasting precious time, but he wanted to delay finding out something bad about his mom.

"My number came up first on her records, and I said I'd call you. Want me to go down there with you?"

"No, it's Christmas. You need to spend it with your family."

"Since Joan died, it's just the kids and me, and we had our Christmas last night."

"Thanks, Doc, but I'll be okay. I'll let you know what I find out unless the hospital calls you first again."

"If you're sure. If you need me after you get there, you have only to say the word."

"I know, and I appreciate it."

He looked up at Mrs. Reno. Whatever was the look on his face, it reflected on hers, because she laid her hand on his arm. "You need to go. Now."

He nodded. "Tell Mandy I'll call her later."

"I will—and we'll finish that conversation another time. We'll say a special prayer for your mama."

THE ROAD to Madisonville never felt so long. He called and got an update, in case he needed to use the lights on his Jeep to clear the way and get there faster.

She'd stabilized, finally, after they gave her a blood thinner to reduce the risk of stroke. He didn't call his grandparents. There was no reason for them to trek down there if she was stable. He'd call when he knew more, and would see that they got there if anything ... happened.

He squeezed the steering wheel and stiffened his arms.

God, she's too young for this. I still need her.

When he got to the entrance of the hospital, he rushed up to her room to see several people working on her.

One of the nurses approached him as he came in the door. "Sir, you need to go to the waiting room."

"I'm her son."

She brooked no argument. "If you stand in the way here, it could mean your mother's life.

He stood outside the door, leaning on the wall, praying, listening to what they were saying.

Pulling out his phone, he called Doc Boyd. "Doc, it's Clay."

"What's going on, Clay, didn't think you'd be there yet."

"I called on the way, and she'd stabilized, and now they're all in there working on her. She may have coded."

"I'll be there in a half-hour."

"Thanks, Doc."

"Don't thank me, yet. I had an idea after I talked to you earlier. I want to talk it over with the doctor there."

Clay nodded, knowing Doc couldn't see him on the other end of the phone.

"Keep praying, Clay."

"Sure thing, Doc."

He took a deep breath and raised his eyes to the ceiling, praying out loud, unconscious of anyone around him, the pain in his chest almost bringing him to his knees. "Are You there, God? Can You save my mom? Are You in the healing business anymore? Is this how it's going to be from now on? Please God, no."

The nurse who'd shooed him out the door put a hand on his arm to get his attention. "Mr. Lacey, you can come in now."

So, this is it. He closed his eyes briefly. Mom would expect him to face this like a man.

"Is she gone?"

A horror-stricken look crossed her face. "Oh, no, Mr. Lacey, her heart rate is normalizing and she's awake. You can come in and see her now."

The relief at those words had no bounds. "Thank you." He turned quickly, going into the hospital room. "Mom?"

She smiled weakly. "I'm okay, Clay."

"I don't know as I'd go that far."

"Well, better than I was a little while ago." A stricken look crossed her face. "Oh, Clay, you're supposed to be at the Christmas Eve service." Tears trickled from her eyes.

She thought it was still yesterday. It concerned him, but he didn't want to upset her.

"Mom, don't you know that I'd be here no matter what?"

"I just don't want to get in the way of you having a life of your own." She sniffed, blowing her nose on the tissue he handed her.

"Let's worry about one thing at a time, okay? Right now, it's you I'm concerned about, so that's covered."

"I've never felt this way before. Jittery and sluggish at the same time. When I've taken over-the-counter PM meds before, they didn't do this."

She was sticking to her story that she hadn't intended to overdose. He'd have to go along with it until he could talk to the doctor and ask him why she was confused about the date.

"I know, Mom. Doc Boyd is on his way too."

She became agitated. "Oh, Clay, you didn't need to drag him out on Christmas Eve, of all times. He has his children to his house on Christmas Eve."

"He insisted." Clay looked up as the ER doctor entered with another nurse.

"You're Mrs. Lacey's son?"

"Yes. Can you tell me anything?

"We're monitoring her heart, and we'll do an ultrasound of her carotids as soon as the technician comes up. We're a little short-staffed for the holidays."

TWO MINUTES until time for the exceedingly long-distance call from Mom and Dad in Brazil. Mandy made sure the cable from the computer to the television was working and had the camera affixed to the top of the wide-screen television so that when they looked at her parents on the screen, they would be looking toward them instead of to the side.

Everyone was arranged on the couch and the floor so that they could be seen, including the newest member of the family, two-month-old baby Chloe, whom the grandparents had only met via technology. They had planned to be back in plenty of time for her birth, but the South American natural disaster messed up a lot of travel and family plans. Mandy knew Mom was getting worried that they might miss the arrival of Rob and Ella's little one as well.

She was trying not to think about Clay's rushed exit earlier. Every time she thought about it, she said a little prayer for his mom and his safety.

Mandy's phone started buzzing with the call. "It's them!" She bustled over to the computer and answered the call.

"Are you there?" Mom and Dad appeared on the screen, Mom leaning over to make sure they were connected, her face distorted when she got too close to the camera on the laptop.

Mandy chuckled. "We're here, Mom. Lean back so we can see Dad." After she got things set up, she went back to her spot in front of the couch, with the "littles."

"Oh, it's so good to see all of you together." Were those

tears in Mom's eyes? "I've been so sad to miss Christmas with you all."

"We're doing great, Mom." Mandy felt a little hiccup in the region of her heart, her earlier sadness coming back to a degree. "We've had Christmas dinner, but we're saving some of the gifts to open when you get back."

"You didn't have to do that." Dad swiped his hand across his nose and leaned forward. "Let me see everybody." He adjusted his bifocals and gazed at all of them, then smiled. "I thought Clay was going to be there?"

Mandy frowned. Why would he think that? "He was, earlier. His mom is in the hospital, and there was an emergency."

"Oh, I hope everything's okay." Dad paused. "Tell him I enjoyed talking to him the other day."

A jolt of surprise hit her. Hard.

Wait. Clay talked to Dad?

Mandy frowned a little when she saw Mom's exasperated look when she elbowed Dad in the ribs. Mom looked into the camera. "Tell Clay we'll be praying for Diane."

Grandma spoke up quickly. "Christine, we did the best we could, but we know now who the Christmas elf in the family is."

Mom blinked a few times, then got back on track. "Thank you, Sylvia. That's nice of you to say."

Mandy had stayed quiet, trying to figure out why Dad mentioned talking to Clay. She was pondering this while conversations were going on around them. The grandkids were busy holding up the gifts Santa brought, to show their grandparents, and they all talked over one another until Dad held up his hands and said, "Whoa!" and made them go, one at a time, so they'd each have a bit of their grandparents' attention.

Maybe she would have a chance to talk to him later.

She tried to get her head back in the long-awaited Christmas call, but she was distracted, and more than a little curious. Thankfully they had Chloe to *ooh* and *aah* over.

They hadn't even asked about her mysterious benefactor.

Curiouser and curiouser.

Chapter 16

When Doc Boyd arrived, Diane looked more than a little relieved to see him.

"You didn't have to come all the way down here. I'm fine." Mom's color was up, which seemed like a good thing.

Doc took the hand that didn't have an IV needle in it, settling in the chair Clay had vacated to welcome him. "I can't think of any place I'd rather be, Diane."

"But your kids. Your grandkids."

"I was with them last night, so today I'm all yours."

Mom frowned slightly but blushed when she looked at the gentleman sitting next to her. Looking out the window, her eyes widened. "It's daylight."

"Merry Christmas, Diane." Doc Boyd took her hand and squeezed it.

"It's Christmas?" She looked around, realizing, Clay thought, for the first time since the episode, that she wasn't in the Crittenden Community Hospital ER. She looked up, confused. "Clay?"

"You're in Madisonville, in the hospital."

Pulling her hand from Doc's, she closed her eyes, her previously rosy face turning ashen. "I don't understand." Looking from Clay to Doc Boyd, she stiffened her jaw. "I did not try to hurt myself."

Her heart monitor started beeping, and a nurse came in. "Mrs. Lacey, you've got to stay calm until we figure out what's going on with you."

Taking a deep breath, she nodded. "I've been pretty out of it, haven't I?"

Doc reached for her again. "You have, but we're going to get to the bottom of it." He sent a tremulous smile her way. "I promise."

"You said you'd had some thoughts about what's going on with Mom?" Clay was glad to have a familiar face, a comforting presence in the hospital room. Yes, he had God, always, in the form of the Holy Spirit, but Doc's familiar easy-going manner was soothing to both Laceys in the room.

"I'm going to suggest they run tests on your thyroid." Reluctantly, it seemed to Clay, Doc let go of Mom's hand and turned to him as the hospitalist came in. "I looked over her blood work again, and there were some inconsistencies."

Clay nodded, hopeful.

The young man in scrubs held out his hand. "I'm Doctor Hawkins."

"Doctor Boyd, and this is Clay, Mrs. Lacey's son."

"Glad to see you, Doctor." He opened the chart in his hand. We'd like to run some tests on her carotid arteries. Rule out stroke."

Doc nodded. "That's good, but can I make a request as her family doctor?"

"Of course."

"I'm going to suggest they take pictures of her thyroid while they're in the neighborhood."

WHILE HIS MOM was getting X-rays, Clay and Doc Boyd walked slowly and quietly down the hall to the lobby and sat down.

"Doc, do you think she tried to commit suicide?" Clay had to ask. Had to know.

The Doctor pinned him with a look. "No, Clay, I do not."

Clay looked down. How does he know? Isn't mental illness hereditary? "Why do you feel so certain?"

After a pause and a deep breath, Doc spoke. "Because I've known your mother for a long time, been her doctor for a long time. I've seen people who were suicidal, and your mother isn't. If she were, it would have happened before now." Doc shrugged. "It's a gut instinct, I guess."

Encouraging, but could he trust Doc's gut?

"So, you think there's more going on than depression? Can thyroid issues have symptoms like she's had?"

"It absolutely can." Doc leaned forward, turning toward Clay. "I've been researching thyrotoxicosis."

"Say again?" Clay almost laughed. "Is that even a word?"

Doc grinned. "Yes, young man, it is. It's caused by an over-abundance of thyroid hormone in the body, and can cause many of the symptoms Diane has experienced."

Clay took a deep breath. "I don't want to get my hopes up."

"I understand." Doc turned to face Clay, looked down, then up at him as if he wanted to say something and didn't quite know how to put it. "Clay ... I—" He cleared his throat. "I'd like to take your mother to dinner sometime when she gets to feeling better. If it's okay with you, that is?"

Laughter and relief bubbled up inside Clay. If Doc wanted to date his mother, then he must not think she was crazy *or* dying. But Mom? Dating? She always said she'd already had the love of her life. Doc had been a widower for a few years and had a happy marriage before illness claimed his wife too soon. He'd noticed, however, that Mom seemed to light up a little when Doc was in the room. She didn't seem to mind his taking her hand, either.

"You want to date my mom?" Clay felt his lips twitching.

Doc scratched his head and grinned, face flushed. "I guess I do. Hadn't really thought of it as *dating*, but now that you mention it ..."

Clay couldn't think of a better man in whom to trust his mother. He put out his hand. "Permission granted."

WHEN MOM GOT BACK into her room, feeling much better, Clay decided to leave them to their own devices when Doc mentioned wanting to watch a Christmas program on television with her.

This day went from one extreme to another.

Now, back at the Reno household, which was still full of people from earlier, Clay obeyed Grandma Reno when this time she specifically asked him to follow her into the kitchen.

Grandma stopped to refrigerate what had, that morning, been a twenty-pound turkey, and turned. "All right, Clay, I'll ask you the same question I asked earlier today. Just what are your intentions toward my granddaughter?"

Now, he was trapped, hands full of dishes after a second sitting of Christmas supper at the Reno's house, by a diminutive septuagenarian in her own kitchen. *Her turf.* He finally got up the nerve to look at her face. She seemed pleased. *That's a relief. Maybe.*

Swallowing thickly, he found the words he hadn't

verbalized to anyone but God, and had begun to think would never be said aloud. "I think I'd like to get to know her better."

"Seems to me like you know her pretty well, considering how well you did on your little 'Twelve Days of Christmas' campaign." She chuckled. "I'd say you've got a leg up on anybody else, once she knows who it is."

"That's the problem. I don't think she thinks of me that way."

"And what *way* is that?" Mrs. Reno narrowed her eyes at him.

"Well, in a ... romantic sort of way?" He wanted to groan at his inability to say what he wanted.

This is so embarrassing.

Mandy's Grandma took the dishes from his hands and set them on the table, then took his hands in hers, forcing him to look her in the eye. "Clay Lacey, you know I love you, don't you?"

He nodded. There had never been a time in his life that he didn't know the Reno family. He'd always felt close to them, even after he no longer pursued their other granddaughter, Lisa. He was a little short on family, and they knew it. "I do."

"Then believe me when I tell you this. I'd have been tickled pink if Lisa had married you, but I never thought it felt quite ... right. For either one of you. But now? I've kept my eyes open. I see how you look at her, and how she looks at you."

This was like getting a blessing Clay hadn't expected.

Grandma continued. "Don't wait too long to let her know it was you. Her daddy just about let the cat out of the bag when we talked this afternoon." Grandma shook her head. "My son. I've been telling him all his life that his mouth was going to get him in trouble. Good thing he was a teacher and got to talk for a living." Clay felt his hands being squeezed by her smaller, wrinkled ones. He met her eyes. She was serious. "But Clay, whatever was in that card touched her heart."

"It was just a quote from Emerson."

"Well, I don't know my Emerson from anybody else in the literary world, but it was well chosen."

"Thank you."

"For what?"

"For not thinking I'm too old for her."

She let go of his hands and shook her head, whacking him on his arm. "You are not too old, you hear me?"

He chuckled. "I hear you."

"And if anybody says anything, they'll have me to deal with."

"Yes, ma'am." He picked up a dishrag and winked at her as he went back into the dining room.

Chapter 17

The "littles," as Mandy called them, were all either asleep, playing quietly, or engrossed in a holiday cartoon in the den while the adults played some games and talked. It was the calm after the storm.

Clay had heard about the call that almost got him outed, and he noticed Mandy watching him quietly with a question in her eyes. He had hoped she would guess he was her secret Santa, Christmas Stalker, whatever, but at the same time, he was fearful. What if it didn't turn out that what was wrong with Mom was thyroid issues? What if mental illness ran in their family?

When he found the Emerson quote, he was astounded. He had looked for a scripture that fit the season, but when he found "My Wish for You," he had to use it. Every statement was true to what he hoped for Mandy, whether it included him or not.

The most recent card game over, Grandpa was snoring in his recliner, and Cassie's husband Brad was dozing on one end of the sofa. An infant in the house meant little sleep, from what he'd heard. What would it be like to have three kids? Rob was the same age as him, and expecting number three any time now. Cassie fed Chloe as she and Grandma sat at the dining table, looking at a photo album of Christmases past.

It was a comfortable lull.

Mandy sat, cross-legged, on the floor next to the coffee table, next to the chair where Clay sat. His fingers itched to touch her, so close he could reach out and run them through her hair.

If he dared.

And he didn't.

She'd been quiet ever since he'd returned. Not a sad quietness, but one of thoughtful consideration.

He watched as she absently rubbed the silver bracelet. It was the one he'd given her on the second day of Christmas. She looked up at him, a solemn look on her face. "Would you like to go for a walk?"

He caught her gaze with his own, then looked out the window at the gathering twilight. "It's starting to get dark. How about a drive, instead?"

"That works. If the kids were older, we could take them to see Christmas lights, but there would be too many car seats to manage at this stage." She twisted her lips in a smile. "I think we need to talk."

He couldn't say anything, so he nodded and stood, unconsciously reaching down to give her a hand up from the floor. When she took it and hoisted herself up right in front of him, he felt a lump of nervous anticipation in his throat that he hadn't felt in a very long time. *Is this a mistake? Does she want to let me down easily?*

Mandy walked into the dining room, avoiding her

grandfather and brother. "Grandma, Clay and I are going for a drive. We'll be back in a little while."

"All right, sweetie. We can have dessert again when you get back if you're hungry."

Mandy kissed her on the cheek and grinned. "I might eat some more dressing—don't heat it up."

"I know. You like it cold, right out of the refrigerator." Sylvia Reno shook her head and chuckled.

Cassie frowned at her little sister. "I never could figure out why you like it that way."

"I don't know, either, but I do." She looked up at Clay. "Ready?"

He held her coat as she put it on, then led the way to his vehicle.

WAS CLAY HER SECRET ADMIRER? Mandy was in a quandary. Part of her wanted desperately for it to be him. Part of her was irritated that the whole community had pulled one over on her.

"Are you warm enough?" Clay looked over from the driver's side. "I can turn up the thermostat."

"I'm fine." She settled in, wriggling a little and sighing at the comfort of the Jeep. "I hope you don't have seat warmers in the back seat."

He laughed, sounding relieved. Was he as nervous as she? "Why's that?"

"Criminals don't deserve this delicious warmth." She snuggled down in the leather seats, the heat relaxing her, giving her the courage to say what she needed to say. Ask what she needed to ask.

"I'll keep that in mind." He drove for a minute or so, a thoughtful smile on his face. "And, by the way, the back seats don't have them."

"Only fair."

"I agree." They drove on, winding down State Road 91 toward Marion. "I guess you're wondering why I talked to your dad."

"I was." She looked at him closely. "Wondering, that is."

He took a deep breath. "A few years ago, I made a fool of myself when I asked Lisa to marry me."

"Well, it *was* at the cemetery where she'd just buried her mother." She'd felt sorry for him that day, but this far out, it did have its humorous side. He was much younger.

He grimaced. "Exactly. Since then, I reconciled myself to the fact that maybe God didn't have that kind of relationship in mind for me."

She frowned. "What does that have to do with you talking to my dad?"

He didn't say anything, but pulled into the spot marked "Sheriff" in the courthouse parking lot and put the Jeep in park.

"Let's walk around the courthouse and see the lights."

He went around to open the door for her, pulling the hood of her jacket up to ward off the cold. Clay pushed his hands into his coat pockets and started walking, not saying anything. They got around to the front of the courthouse where the trees were filled with lights, a nativity sat front and center, and Santa on a tractor finished the quirky small-town decorating.

Mandy looked over at the other side of Marion's Main Street, then up and down at the streetlights and houses tastefully illuminated. It was beautiful. Peaceful. Not one vehicle had come by since they'd been here.

Somehow, it all made sense. She didn't believe in

coincidence. Roxy had spilled that her benefactor was not a relative, and Clay was the only person outside of the family with whom she'd shared her frustration about her parents not being able to come home for Christmas. He was the only one outside of her family and Caryn who knew she was hurting, and he had been there for her every step of the way.

A few random snowflakes floated gently to the ground. Was this God telling her something? In the South, as special as Christmas was on its own, snow always made it feel magical, as if anything could happen.

Tears pricked at her eyelids. There she went again. She was going to have to have a talk with those tear ducts. Lawyers were tough. They didn't wear their hearts on their sleeves. Did they? She got up the nerve to look at him.

He had turned toward her, looking down with an expression that she'd caught glimpses of from time to time, but just put it down to the fact that he was a very nice man who cared about the people around him.

"Mandy —"

"Clay, it was you."

They both spoke at the same time. Clay's eyes rounded at the ease with which she made her pronouncement, and nodded.

"Guilty."

MANDY'S LIPS lifted in a smile. "It's the nicest thing anyone has ever done for me." She reached out to touch his arm. "Really."

"You were sad, and I had an idea to help you feel better." He shrugged, wondering if he could possibly tell her the real "Why" of Operation Twelve Days of Mandy Reno. Had it really only taken him a little over twelve days to fall in love with her?

When he finally admitted it to himself, the reality jolted him to a stop.

Maybe he'd been noticing her all along. When had he begun thinking of her as a "warrior princess"? He'd always admired her confidence and self-control. Fearless. When they were all kids, he and Rob hung out, and there was Mandy, trying to get in on whatever they were doing—but he never seemed to mind. He thought maybe he was just jealous that Rob had a sister and he didn't. Lisa was closer to his age and seemed to be the obvious choice for him.

Had he been focusing on the wrong Reno all along?

"Why did you call my dad?" Mandy held him still with her gaze. She was calm, cool, and collected, but her heightened color made him wonder—or was she just cold?

He tilted his head. In for a penny, in for a pound. "I called your dad because I wasn't sure he would approve."

"Approve of what?" She wasn't going to let him off easy. She'll be a great lawyer.

"Me. And you."

She stood there, waiting, not saying anything, but her look kept softening as the seconds, which felt like minutes or hours, passed.

Clay dove in. "If he didn't approve of my asking you out, I wasn't going to do it. I'd have let this go by and not tell you." He looked beyond her and snorted. "You'd have figured it out eventually because half the county was in on it."

She felt the tears begin to fall as she laughed. "Dad said to tell you he enjoyed talking to you. What's that mean, you think?"

And now he was afraid to look at her.

"Clay."

Finally, he turned his gaze to her, startled at her tears. "Why are you crying?"

Had he messed up royally?

"Because I think we're both going to die of old age before you get around to asking me out for a date."

Chapter 18

He felt his smile grow wider with relief, and his hand came up to cover hers as it rested on his arm. His heart leaped, but he narrowed his eyes to disguise the emotion he felt. "Do *the kids* go on *dates* these days?"

"I don't really know. I've always hung around with the old folks, you know." She laughed at the expression on his face. "I'm not including you in that category." She gave him a narrow look. "I'm not quite sure how I feel about your asking my dad's permission to date me. I am twenty-four years old, you know."

He sobered. "I know. It hit me like a ton of bricks when I realized."

"What?"

"That you were old enough to consider dating someone my age." He shook his head. "Honestly, it scared me to death."

"Really?" She looked at him closely. "I don't see any gray hair." She looked around where they stood. "Did you forget your cane?" Then she laughed.

"All right, so the lawyer is a comedienne." He chuckled

with her, then sobered, using his free hand to tuck a stray strand of her dark hair behind her ear. She bit her lip and it did something to him. "God has three possible answers to every prayer."

"Yes, no, or wait." She turned her hand in his and wove her fingers with his.

His heart was beating like a tom-tom, and he wondered if this was what a heart attack felt like.

Would he survive this?

When he looked into her luminous eyes, he shook his head incredulously. "I never knew what that *wait* was for until you."

When her eyes widened and she caught her breath suddenly, he couldn't wait any longer. He leaned down and kissed her tender lips. They were every bit as soft as he thought they would be. Her hand pulled from his and landed on his cheek. His hand felt empty, but the rest of him was humming along nicely. Hood down, he threaded his now-free hand through her dark brown hair, finally able to feel the silky tresses for himself as he wanted to earlier.

God had said, "Wait," and he had. He waited, and it was worth it.

Mandy Reno would always be worth it.

He pulled back to look at her, noting her eyes seemed a little unfocused, and he smiled. The exhilaration of finally being here, in this place, at just this time, made him feel ten feet tall.

She reached up and kissed him softly, then whispered to him, "You still haven't asked me."

"Asked you what?" All he wanted to know was when he could kiss her again. Now, maybe?

She put her fingers to his lips when he would go for more of the sweetness she offered. "Ask me."

It dawned on him that they had talked all around the

subject of him asking her out on a date. It was almost like they'd skipped to date two or three since he'd been thinking of her almost constantly for the last few weeks.

He tightened his hold on her, pulling her as close as possible, looking her square in the face in all seriousness. "Amanda Lou Reno, will you go on a date with me?"

She burst out laughing. "Finally. I would love to go on a date with you—as long as you never call me Amanda Lou again."

The thrill that coursed through his veins at this simple answer was all he needed, and he could think of one time in the future, hopefully, that he would call her Amanda Lou again. He pulled her into an embrace, simply holding her, and she tucked her head under his chin. Was it cliché of him to marvel at how she fit perfectly in his arms?

She pulled back suddenly, a frown creasing her brow. "I have a question for *you*, now."

He twisted his lips. "Ask away."

"What in the world does OTDMR stand for?"

Clay laughed and kissed her again. "Operation Twelve Days of Mandy Reno."

Her smile grew. "Perfect. I like it."

"You approve, huh?"

"Definitely." Her brow raised. "We might have to celebrate OTDMR every year."

"I think that can be arranged." He could get behind the idea of making Mandy Reno happy every Christmas for the rest of his life. Pulling her closer, she settled into his arms, her head resting on his chest.

"Merry Christmas, Clay." Her voice was muffled in his coat.

"Merry Christmas, Mandy." He lifted her chin with his finger and captured her lips once more.

Clay was sure all the people at her grandparents' house

were wondering what kept them. They'd have to go back eventually, but now? Now he wanted to revel in the fact that the prettiest girl in Clementville—no, in the world—had agreed to go out with him.

For now, that was enough. He had a feeling that after this, Christmas would never be the same.

Operation Twelve Days of Mandy Reno was a success.

THE END

Recipe: House of Grace
Sweet Tea

Equipment

- 1-gallon pitcher
- measuring cups- dry and liquid
- 1 immersion blender

Ingredients

- 3/4 C lemonade mix we use Country Time, sweetened
- 2 C sugar
- 1/2 C instant tea, unsweetened we use decaffeinated tea
- 1 C white grape juice
- 1 gallon water
- lemon wedges and/or fresh mint, optional-add to glasses for serving

Instructions

- Measure dry ingredients and add to a one-gallon pitcher.
- Add white grape juice.
- Fill the pitcher with water to make a gallon.
- Use an immersion blender to stir ingredients completely.
- Chill and serve over ice with lemon wedges and/or fresh mint.

Notes

Curtis Grace and his wife, Norma, were catering and restaurant legends while living and shared this "House of Grace Tea" recipe with our local newspaper. Although the 9th Street House restaurant has been closed since 1996, Curtis and Norma Grace's 9th Street House legacy continues through its recipes and cookbooks.

<hr>

Author's Note

<hr>

Dear Reader,

I hope you enjoyed a visit with the extended Reno family and the fictional community of Clementville, KY, close to where I've lived for over thirty years in Crittenden County, Kentucky—a county where there are more deer than people.

After *Heart Restoration*, book 1 in the RenoVations Inc. series, I felt sorry for Sheriff Clay Lacey, so I decided to give him a story and romance of his own—enter the Reno family and a situation only a secret admirer could handle.

If you'd like to read a prequel to the RenoVations Inc. series, go to my website at www.reginaruddmerrick.com and sign up for my newsletter! You'll receive a pdf copy of the story, *RenoVating Christmas*, where you'll meet many of the characters in Clementville. I'm excited to share this with you.

Clementville is fictional, but based on a true story that took place here. The location of fictional Clementville is located in the very real area between the Cave-In-Rock ferry landing on the Kentucky side of the Ohio River, and Riverfront Park, which is where the old "Dam 50" was located.

It's a beautiful part of the county with rolling hills and river views. The families in the thriving Amish community run greenhouses, cabinetmaking shops, stores, bakeries, and other businesses. Need a saddle repaired? A dozen giant glazed donuts? Plants? New kitchen cabinets? This community can fix you right up.

For Mandy's eleventh gift, Clay arranged to have a flute ensemble perform "Still, Still, Still," a beautiful Christmas song that may be unfamiliar to many. If you want to hear a recording of this that helped inspire that particular gift choice, go to https://www.youtube.com/watch?v=DU8Gm6B3Ro4 .

I hope you enjoy this glimpse into my home county and the lives of the Reno family, and I pray that you have a truly blessed Christmas!

Thank you for reading,

Regina Rudd Merrick

Psalm 37:4

P.S. Stay tuned for an excerpt of Del Reno's story in Book 3 in the RenoVations Inc. series, *Rebuilding Joy*!

Acknowledgments

In any writing project, there are many to thank.

First, I want to thank my husband, Todd, for his love, encouragement, and willingness to loan me to my fictional characters when I need to get away from real people to meet deadlines. I have been so blessed. This revision was completed while taking on a part-time interim librarian job, continued renovations to our home, and death in the family.

My grown-up daughters and son-in-law – Ellen, Emily, and Ben – for their patience and love. By the way, they're all writers too!

My many writing friends and the staff at Scrivenings Press – I love you all so much. You have no idea how wonderful it is to have you to run things by. Sometimes my questions even sound silly to me, but I've never heard that from any of you!

And most of all, to the Father who created us; to my Lord and Savior, Jesus Christ, whose birth we celebrate at Christmas, and the reason for the season we hold so dear; and to the Holy Spirit who is our comforter. Through it all, He gives His peace, His love, and His rest.

Thank you, Heavenly Father, and Merry Christmas!

About the Author

Regina Merrick began reading romance and thinking of book ideas as early as her teenage years when she attempted a happily-ever-after sequel to *Gone With the Wind*. That love of fiction parlayed into a career as a librarian, and ultimately as a full-time writer. She began attending local writing workshops and continued to hone her craft by writing several short and novel-length fan-fiction pieces published online, where she met other authors with a similar love for story, a Christian worldview, and happily-ever-after. After winning a publishing contest with a new publishing company, she realized a dream she never knew she had—the dream of publication.

Married for forty years and active in their church, Regina and her husband have two grown daughters who share her love of music, writing, and the arts, and a son-in-law who loves to ride his bike for unreasonable, to me, distances.

The small town of Marion, Kentucky, thirty minutes from the nearest Wal-Mart, has been home for over thirty years.

Connect with Regina through her website at https://www.reginaruddmerrick.com, Facebook, Instagram, Goodreads, and Bookbub.

Heart Restoration

RenoVations Inc.—Book One

For interior designer Lisa Reno things go from bad to worse when her contractor-brother falls off a ladder and breaks his leg. Now she has to deal with the past coming back to haunt her, an old house with a corpse in the creepy cellar, and her best friend trying her best to fix her up with any man that moves.

Nick Woodward is willing to do his old college roommate a favor–especially since it involves renovating his own inheritance. The last thing he wants is to get involved with anyone. When he lost his wife and unborn child so suddenly, he had made the decision to keep God and everyone else at arm's length. So far, so good.

Ah, the difference a trip to a dingy basement makes.

Get your copy here:

https://scrivenings.link/heartrestoration

Rebuilding Joy

RenoVations Inc.—Book Three

A waitress, a contractor, and an FBI agent walk into a café …

Single mom Darcy Emerson Sloan has enough to do raising twins and running a restaurant. She's doing fine on her own and doesn't need the complications of a man in her life. But when her café turns into a crime scene, putting her and her children in danger, she begins to take interest in the handsome young FBI agent that comes on the scene.

Contractor Del Reno is as even-keeled as they come, but even he has his limits. And Darcy Sloan has pushed him too far. Every time he tries to help, it backfires. But now that Darcy and her kids are in trouble, he has no choice but to come to her aid and protect her. She's just going to have to deal with it.

Secret tunnels, organized crime, adorable children, and a wedding.

Just another day in Clementville.

Coming in February 2024

Rebuilding Joy - Chapter One

May

The sounds of the café receded into the background as a tide of feelings washed over her.

I can do this.

Darcy Emerson Sloan closed her eyes and forced the knot in her chest to subside. Tears were near the surface, but she refused to let her mom know how inadequate she felt to take on the responsibility of the café.

Especially today.

By herself.

Alone.

As the owner-manager.

Mom deserved a break. She'd opened the café when Dad died, using his life insurance money to build a business that made her a successful businesswoman. She and Darcy would much rather have had Dad, but it had been a good life for them.

And now it was Darcy's turn to be in charge.

When Mom married Steve Reno a year ago, after being a widow for fifteen years, she had started talking to Darcy about the possibility of her taking over the business. She'd been proud of the work her daughter had done while she and Steve were on their extended honeymoon trip to Alaska. It was a gift —a gift from her Mom and her late father. For her, she reasoned, the café had seen her through tough times and taken her mind off the indescribable pain of losing a husband unexpectedly.

But I'm not Mom.

"Sweetie?" Roxy Reno, her mom, touched Darcy's arm. "Are you okay?"

She opened her eyes and smiled, coming back to the present. It was a little wobbly, she was sure, but it was there.

I always smile.

"I'm okay, Mom." No one had to know that under the guise of "I'm good, how 'bout you?" Darcy was hurting. That her feelings of inadequacy were rooted deep, through no fault of anyone. It was just her and the stuff life had thrown at her. "Biscuits are in the oven, bacon is cooking, and eggs are broken and ready."

Mom looked at her closely, realization and sadness dawning on her face. "Oh, Darcy. I'm so sorry."

Darcy had trouble meeting her eyes, and it would be time to open the café any minute now. She couldn't go out there and wait on people with tears running down her face, but she wanted to. "About what?" She lifted her chin defiantly, continuing to roll silverware into paper napkins. It was a nice, mindless task.

"I know what today is." Mom clutched her arm, forcing her to glance up. "Look at me, sweetie."

"It's fine, Mom. I'll be okay." She gave a short burst of laughter. Bitterness came through. "Stewing about it won't change a thing, will it?"

Four years. Four years since the sergeant in a Class A uniform had knocked at her door with news no Army wife wanted to hear. When the dreaded news came that Justin wasn't coming back, she was seven months pregnant. A product of Justin's last leave and a quick trip to Hawaii for their second anniversary.

"There's stewing, and then there's grieving." Mom's eyes held the tears Darcy should be shedding, probably. But she couldn't. Not today. "It's okay to grieve."

Darcy shook her head. "Can't. Don't have time." She took a deep breath and looked her mother in the eye. "Is Mandy working today?"

Mom glanced at the clock hanging over the order window and nodded. "She'll be here at seven-thirty."

"Good. Looks like good weather for fishing, so we may have a breakfast rush." If there was one thing Darcy didn't want to talk about, today of all days, it was her feelings, a black hole she had no intention of exploring. Not today.

"I can stay. I should have thought. Let me do this for you."

"Mom, I'm fine. If I'm going to be running the place, you're going to have to give me the chance to take care of things no matter what's going on. Right?" She stared her mother down, trying hard not to grit her teeth. "Wasn't that what you had to do?"

She has more tears in her eyes than I do. Aw Mom, cut it out.

"Besides, you and Steve haven't had a day to call your own in ages, and here you are, checking to make sure the biscuits are made." She grinned. "You newlyweds have to have your time alone, don't you?"

Mom smirked. "Watch it, young lady." She heaved a sigh, looking at the clock again. Their outing was business-related, as usual with Steve Reno, but he'd promised his wife a little fun along the way. "If you're sure. Steve would understand, you know."

"I know he would, and I love him for it. Really, I do. It'll be good for me to stay busy." She reached out to hug her mom and then backed off to look her in the eye. "Jimmy's here to take care of the short-order menu for breakfast, and I'll wait tables until Mandy gets here. When the next shift gets settled in, I'll start making the bread and Jimmy can help me with the lunch prep."

"Sounds like you've got it all under control." Mom's eyes were moist. "I'm proud of you, you know."

Darcy shook her head. "I'm not sure why, but it's a nice thought."

"You really don't know, do you?"

"Know what?"

"That you are a special young lady and you can do whatever you set your mind to."

From your mouth to God's ears. But then, I'd have to trust in a living God for that to work, wouldn't I?

DEL RENO LOOKED in the rearview mirror, took off his cap, and smoothed his hair back before he entered the café.

I need a haircut.

No time for that today. He was supposed to meet Nick at seven thirty, and he was running a few minutes late.

Nick's truck was already parked on the street in front of the building, so the plan was to get breakfast, consult with the tenant—in this case, Darcy—and then get to work. He paused for a moment before entering and closed his eyes. He had imagined he could smell bacon cooking from his house just up the road, but here? Here, it was a siren call in the aromatic sense.

RenoVations Inc. had been hired by the owner, Roxy Reno, to remodel the apartment above the Clementville Café for her daughter, Darcy, and the twins. The apartment atop the pre-war building—*but which war?*—was located on the single strip of businesses in the tiny town of Clementville, Kentucky. It had been empty from the time Roxy remarried last summer until last fall when Darcy and the children moved in. He frowned a bit. He'd never had a problem with the idea of Roxy living above the café, but Darcy and the kids? She was taking too many chances. The nearest neighbor was a few streets away, and she lived ten miles from the county seat in Marion and the nearest law enforcement.

Not that I have any say in the matter.

He shook his head and pulled the sparkling glass door open, setting off jangling bells. At the sound, the waitress—in this case, his cousin Mandy—was alerted.

She raised her hand in a friendly wave. "Hey, Del."

"Hey, Mandy." He grinned at his youngest cousin. She was of average height and only came up to his shoulder. "Nick here yet?"

"Yep. He stepped back to the kitchen to ask Darcy something. I'm assuming about the renovation upstairs. She's minding the ship today."

"Gotcha." He followed her to the counter, nodding as she poured him a cup of coffee.

"The usual?" His cousin raised an eyebrow and put a hand on her hip.

Del eyed her over the menu. "Are you saying I'm predictable?"

"Uh, yeah." She cocked her head to one side. "Two eggs, over easy; an order of bacon, extra-crisp; biscuits and jelly—"

"Hey, sometimes I order gravy."

"Yeah, well, only on special occasions." She continued her list. "And grits."

He twisted his lips, wondering how he could get around this lawyer-wannabe's uncomfortably accurate prediction. Truth was, he loathed his routine and was tired of everyone thinking they knew what was going on in his head. "I might surprise you today." He perused the menu for a moment and, decision made, laid it on the counter. "I think I'll have the pecan waffle, thank you very much."

Mandy laughed. "I'll get your order in, O Great Unpredictable One."

"Thank you." He held up his hand as she moved to walk away, remembering something. "Hey, how was your law school graduation?"

She beamed. Her eyes were sparkling with excitement, but she shrugged casually. "It was okay. The usual long-winded speeches and uncomfortable seats, but wonderful." Wrinkling her nose, she looked apologetic. "I wish I could've invited the whole family, but they only gave me ten tickets, and I wanted Grandma and Grandpa to see their youngest grandchild walk across the platform to get my diploma, and then by the time you add my brother and wife, sister and husband, and some of their kids..."

"And Clay." He quirked a brow, laughing when he saw her face tinged with red.

"And Clay." She took a deep breath and shook her head. "Now I'm studying for the bar exam in July. I waitress to stay sane."

"You'll do great." Del winked at her. "You were always the smartest one in the family, you know."

Mandy leaned over the counter and whispered. "I know, let's keep it our secret."

"What secret?" Nick Woodward scooted onto the stool next to Del. "Good luck. Since becoming a part of the Reno family, I'm learning that in Clementville, you're related to everyone in town, and everybody knows your business, as well." He laughed, clearly not worried about missing a bit of news.

"No big secret, simply confirming what we know to be true. Right, Del?" She winked at Del as he chuckled. "How 'bout some coffee, Nick?"

"Please." He thanked her as she put a mug in front of him and turned to retrieve the carafe.

Del looked around, taking note of Darcy flitting from table to table. He took a sip from his steaming cup of coffee and turned to his best friend and business partner. "How long've you been here?"

"About twenty minutes. Traffic was light between here and Kuttawa." Nick smiled up at Mandy when she filled his cup and put a menu in front of him. "Just give me what Del's having."

"Pecan waffle and syrup?"

Nick turned to Del, his jaw hanging open. "What's wrong with you? You sick or somethin'?"

"I decided I no longer want to be so predictable."

"What's wrong with predictable?" Nick frowned and then looked at Mandy directly. "I'll have waffles too, and a side of bacon."

Del raised a hand. How had he missed bacon? He'd come in dreaming about it. "I'll have bacon, too."

Mandy turned to add the item to Del's ticket and put Nick's on the order wheel between the counter and the kitchen.

"Did you talk to Darcy about the kitchen countertops upstairs?"

"Yeah. She's good with quartz since her mom insisted on it." He lifted one side of his mouth in a grin. "The extra cost made her balk at first, but Roxy won her over. She'll come upstairs to look at samples when she can shake loose." Nick took another sip of his black coffee. "Living here has to be more convenient for her."

The business partners agreed that with two growing preschoolers, she needed the space, and the apartment had square footage, all right.

Del shook his head. "It will be. On the other hand, I hate to think about her hauling the kids up and down those stairs."

Nick chuckled. "I don't think an elevator is in the budget."

"Probably not." Del gave Nick a sidelong glance.

"Besides, Darcy's young. Now when you get to be our age…"

Del glowered at him. "Speak for yourself, old man."

"Hey, you're older than me."

"By two months." Del took a sip and set the cup down when Darcy came up to them with the coffee pot.

"Hey, Del. Need a warm-up?"

Del saw something in her expression. Sadness? "Sure. You doin' okay today, Darcy?"

She took a deep breath like she was trying to shake something off. "Never better."

Del nodded, regarding her closely. She was avoiding him. Something was wrong.

But I have no right to ask her what it is.

NICK COULDN'T HELP but notice the change in atmosphere when Darcy, as opposed to Mandy, walked up to the counter. He shook his head. Del had it so bad, and Nick knew exactly how he felt. He'd been the same way about Del's sister, Lisa Reno, a year ago.

When he and Lisa reconnected after a few years, they'd both lived different lives. Totally different lives. Lisa had temporarily moved to Texas, where she'd had a serious relationship with a guy who, for a time, destroyed her confidence in herself. Nick had married the woman who was, then, the love of his life and lost her and their unborn child to a senseless traffic accident. It had almost destroyed him mentally and spiritually.

Lisa was the one who made him realize God might have more than one love in mind for him. He smiled every time he thought of her and their whirlwind courtship and engagement. Now if they could just speed this wedding thing along. Every week felt like a year.

"Why don't you go ahead and move into your house?" Del was pouring syrup over his pecan waffle. It smelled so good Nick was glad he'd ordered the same thing.

"I promised Lisa I wouldn't move in until I could move in with her, and that she had free rein to fix it up any way she pleased." He shrugged, snorting quietly. "Therefore, I'm still commuting from Kuttawa."

"You are way too nice to her. You know that, don't you?"

Nick laughed. "Probably." He puffed out his chest. "But then, she's worth it."

Del shook his head. "People in love are ridiculous."

"Don't knock it until you've tried it." Nick glanced from Del to Darcy. Seemed as if his old friend Del kept an eye on the lady at all times, and Darcy was studiously indifferent.

Do Del and Darcy think nobody knows? I guess there's hope for even the most stubborn of people.

Del seemed to gather his thoughts. "Anyway, back to the apartment."

"Yeah." Nick took a bite of the luscious pecan waffle dripping in syrup, closing his eyes with pleasure. *Aw, man, these are so good.* "Besides the countertops, I want Darcy to look at the master bath before we do the rough-in plumbing."

"Ripping out the plaster was painful." Del sighed.

"I know. It was the only way to get the layout she needed." Nick stared straight ahead, thinking. "I asked Roxy if she wanted the electrical done now or in phases."

"It's going to be hard to do it in phases if she and the twins are living in it."

"I know. I have a feeling it's going to be full steam ahead, which means they'll have to move out for a few weeks."

"If Dad has anything do to with it—and you know he will—we'll be up to our necks in plaster dust by the end of the week."

Nick laughed. "So much for semi-retirement, huh?"

"The man doesn't know the meaning of the word. Roxy just thinks they're having a day out. His main destination is the supply house in Owensboro." Del scraped the remaining syrup from his plate with the last piece of bacon. "How are the wedding plans coming along?"

Nick held up his hands. "As far as I know, swimmingly. Lisa said she would let me know when she needed my help, which is fine by me. At this point, we both want to have this planning stuff over and be married, already."

"You could always elope, and then I wouldn't have to wear a tux." Del looked at him hopefully.

"You know that's not going to happen." Nick shook his head. "Lisa is worried about leaving anyone out. I told her nobody cares as much as she does, and that just made her mad."

Del laughed out loud, causing Darcy, Mandy, Jimmy in the

kitchen, and several customers to turn their way right about the time the doorbells jangled again.

"Keep it down, man." Nick looked around, embarrassed.

Del tried to stop laughing, but couldn't. "I could have told you that the one thing Lisa Reno can't stand is when you tell her a truth she doesn't want to hear."

"Now you tell me."

LISA RENO JUMPED from the driver's seat of her Ford Explorer and made her way to the door of the café, glad the sun had come up, at least. Poor Nick. He'd had to leave before sunrise. The sunny almost-summer day was a blessing after all the rain they'd had in the last few weeks.

The aroma of baking biscuits and breakfast food reached her before she heard the bell on the door emit a loud "clang," and instead of everyone looking at the door, their attention was on her boys, Nick and Del. She sidled up to her fiancé and kissed him on the cheek, surprising him.

Lisa laughed at the guilty expression on his face. "What?"

"You surprised me, that's all. Good morning." Nick turned and claimed her lips with his, driving all thoughts of questions out of her mind.

Mmmm...Maple syrup...

"What are you guys having for breakfast?" She claimed the stool next to Nick, unrolled her silverware, and placed the napkin in her lap before checking out their nearly-empty plates. "Looks—and tastes—like something that requires syrup, surprise, surprise." She grinned, looking at what little food was left. "Ooh, pecan waffles. Nice choice."

"Hey Lisa, need some coffee?" Mandy was manning the

coffee pot this time while Darcy took orders from customers who had come in right before Lisa.

"Hi, Mandy." She thought for a minute.

Do I have time for a full breakfast? Do I WANT a full breakfast? She sighed. "Yes to the coffee, and I'll just have a sausage and biscuit sandwich."

"Good deal," Darcy said, nodding. "Jimmy made up a bunch for a to-go order and had a few extras. Still fresh."

"Perfect. Thanks." Lisa watched Darcy walk away, wondering.

"How do you run on such a small breakfast?" Del snorted at her order.

"For one thing, my breakfast won't be loaded with sugar, so I won't have a sugar crash around eleven o'clock, and for another, I have a dress fitting tomorrow." She shrugged. "Besides, you're nearly done, and I'd hate to make you wait for me." She winked at Nick and gave her brother, Del, the stink eye, which only made him laugh.

"Who said we were going to wait?"

"I think the 'Reno' in 'RenoVations Inc.' includes me, right?" Lisa smiled when Mandy filled her coffee cup with the steaming elixir. "I may be a coffee snob, but you can say one thing about the coffee here. It's amazing." She took a whiff and then brought the mug to her lips to check the temperature. "Mmmm, perfect."

Darcy presented her sausage biscuit sandwich with a flourish. "Here you go, Lisa. Jimmy's outdone himself in the biscuit department today."

She admired the flaky height of the steaming buttermilk quick bread expertly split to contain the oversized sausage patty, which had been fried to perfection. "I'll say. I hate to bite into it." She held up a finger and then pulled out her phone to take a picture of the masterpiece. "I'll tag you on Instagram."

Darcy laughed. Lisa could sense that something was bothering her, but she didn't want to ask her here in the café.

"Darcy, I have a dress fitting tomorrow. Want to come with me? If you do, it will give me an excuse to eat out and do a little wedding shopping." She cut her eyes at Nick. "And it's for sure that Nick can't go with me, because I don't want him to have any idea what my dress looks like."

Darcy tilted her head, seeming to consider. "What time? I planned to take off a little early tomorrow to do grocery shopping."

"My appointment isn't until four o'clock. We could fit in a supermarket stop." Maybe they'd have a chance to talk.

"I'll see what I can do with the kids. I'd hate to think about my two Tasmanian devils in a bridal shop." Darcy shook her head.

"Hey, that's my niece and nephew you're talking about." Lisa grinned. "I'm sure they'd be fine, but you need some time out, too." She looked at Nick and Del for backup. "Right?"

Del had a thoughtful expression on his face, eyeing Darcy. "I don't mind watching them."

Darcy paused, a tiny frown between her brows. "Are you sure?"

He waved off her concern. "I'll be here working anyway. How hard could it be? I can pick them up at preschool and feed them supper, and then I can take them to my place or come to yours. Whatever works for you?" He seemed worried that she wouldn't accept the offer.

Lisa did a double-take. *He's never babysat kids in his life.*

Darcy was thoughtful. "It would be easier to keep them here at the apartment - all their stuff is here, and they can go to bed earlier. And you have a key." She bit her lip and looked across the counter at Del. "You're sure?"

"Wouldn't have offered if I wasn't."

Lisa stared at her brother. *He wants a shot at this.*

While she was pondering this new development, she watched him shoot Darcy a smile as he got up from the counter and retrieved his check.

"That settles it, then. I will be your babysitter for the evening. I know we'll have a great time."

More Books by Regina Merrick

A Southern Breeze Series:

Carolina Dream

A Southern Breeze Series: Book One

https://scrivenings.link/carolinadream

Carolina Mercy

A Southern Breeze Series: Book Two

https://scrivenings.link/carolinamercy

Carolina Grace

A Southern Breeze Series: Book Three

https://scrivenings.link/carolinagrace

Novella Collections:

Love in Any Season:

A Novella Collection

https://scrivenings.link/loveinanyseason

Candy Cane Wishes and Saltwater Dreams:

A Novella Collection

https://scrivenings.link/candycanewishes

Coastal Promises: